"Oh good," she declared on a relieved sigh. "Looks like we dodged a bullet."

Had he?

His clothes might have been all right, but the hit to his equilibrium rocked him. "I'm Nolan." He'd left off his last name, reluctant to see her open expression slam closed when she realized he was a Thurston.

"Chelsea."

She held out her hand to him. The rough calluses on the palm that connected with his affirmed that this wasn't a woman who sat back and let others do the work. His interest in her flared still brighter, making him regret the animosity between their families.

"I've seen you around town," he said, dipping his toe into the murky situation. "But never dressed like this." He let his appreciation shine as he flicked his gaze along her slim form.

Her husky chuckle raised goose bumps on his arms. The bold interest lighting her eyes twisted up his insides. Lust at first sight wasn't an unfamiliar phenomenon to him, but few women presented the sort of intriguing danger Chelsea Grandin embodied.

* * *

On Opposite Sides by Cat Schield
is part of the Texas Cattleman's Club:
Ranchers and Rivals series.

Dear Reader,

It's always a joy to visit Royal, Texas, and spend some time with the members of the Texas Cattleman's Club families who make these stories so much fun. This time around, I'm delighted to be contributing a story of star-crossed lovers who find themselves on opposite sides of a family feud. An enemies-to-lovers story is one of my favorite tropes both to read and write, especially when the stakes are high.

I love all the drama of the Texas Cattleman's Club books, and this Ranchers and Rivals series has it all. Yet it's the fantastic chemistry between the heroes and heroines that makes these stories so special. I hope you enjoy the romance between Chelsea and Nolan as this pair of opposites figures out what they're willing to risk for love.

Happy reading!

Cat Schield

CAT SCHIELD

—

ON OPPOSITE SIDES

Special thanks and acknowledgment
are given to Cat Schield for her contribution to the
Texas Cattleman's Club: Ranchers and Rivals miniseries.

Recycling programs
for this product may
not exist in your area.

ISBN-13: 978-1-335-73570-6

On Opposite Sides

Copyright © 2022 by Harlequin Enterprises ULC

For questions and comments about the quality of this book, please contact us at CustomerService@Harlequin.com.

Harlequin Enterprises ULC
22 Adelaide St. West, 41st Floor
Toronto, Ontario M5H 4E3, Canada
www.Harlequin.com

Printed in U.S.A.

Cat Schield is an award-winning author of contemporary romances for Harlequin Desire. She likes her heroines spunky and her heroes swoonworthy. While her jet-setting characters live all over the globe, Cat makes her home in Minnesota with her daughter, two opinionated Burmese cats and a goofy Doberman. When she's not writing or walking dogs, she's searching for the perfect cocktail or traveling to visit friends and family. Contact her at www.catschield.com.

Books by Cat Schield

Harlequin Desire

Sweet Tea and Scandal

Upstairs Downstairs Baby
Substitute Seduction
Revenge with Benefits
Seductive Secrets
Seduction, Southern Style

Texas Cattleman's Club: Ranchers and Rivals

On Opposite Sides

Visit her Author Profile page at Harlequin.com, or catschield.com, for more titles!

You can also find Cat Schield on Facebook, along with other Harlequin Desire authors, at Facebook.com/harlequindesireauthors!

For my dad.

One

Chelsea Grandin was proud of the fact that she could outrope, outride and outlast half the men on her family's ranch. Unfortunately, none of her abilities had ever impressed any of the male members of her family. Eldest of her siblings, she had all the first-child traits. An ambitious, responsible know-it-all, she was always the first one out the door in the morning and the last one in the door at night.

Take today, for instance. She'd left the house at 4:00 a.m. so she could get all her work done in order to take off the afternoon for Royal's Fourth of July celebration. With the sun at its zenith, she'd already put in a full day with no sign of her brother, Vic.

"Oh, to be the only boy and presumptive heir," she muttered, wincing as she lost control of her seething resentment. No matter how hard she worked, her father made it clear he intended to turn control of the ranch over to his son. And because of this, Vic behaved like it was his due. "Entitled jerk."

The siblings had different management styles. Chelsea loved working side by side with the ranch hands, believing if she contributed significantly to the daily activity, she was more in tune with the pulse of the ranch. Plus, she took satisfaction in all the physical activity. Vic, in contrast, preferred to delegate. While she wasn't deluded into thinking she was the only person who knew what was going on, Chelsea was convinced she was far more informed than her brother. Not that this had ever given her a leg up when it came to impressing her father or her late grandfather.

Grief gave her heart an agonizing wrench. They'd buried Victor John Grandin Sr. two short months earlier, but Chelsea continued to miss the family's strong patriarch. He'd been such an enormous presence in her life, inspiring her to work ever harder to prove herself, even though the patriarchy was alive and well on the Grandin ranch.

Chelsea slipped out of her truck and approached the front porch, where her sibling sat with his feet up on the railing.

"So I guess you're taking today off," she said, slogging up the steps to the porch, feeling her early morning catching up to her.

"It's the Fourth of July," Vic said, arching one eyebrow at her.

"Your point?" Chelsea hated being constantly irritated with her brother.

Daily she grappled with the certainty that their father would bypass her and hand the reins to Vic. It was just so unfair that being born a girl meant she had no shot at being in charge of the ranch, no matter her qualifications or dedication.

Equally frustrating was the lack of recognition she craved. If she'd been born into another family, she'd be basking in her parents' approval. Instead, both her father and mother saw her contributions as something to keep her occupied until she got married and moved out. They didn't recognize how tied she was to the land her family had owned for generations.

"The point is," Vic began in the unruffled tone that always set her teeth on edge, "today's a holiday, and I'm not working."

As if that explained it all. And maybe it did. With her working so hard, did he really have to?

"No," Chelsea grumbled, "it's not like you're working."

Entering the massive house she shared with her entire family, Chelsea contemplated the moment when Vic took over. How she could possibly stay, knowing that every time they butted heads he would win? Yet the ranch was her everything. What would she do instead?

As Chelsea crossed the spacious living room, her gaze fell on a recent family portrait taken at Layla's engagement party. Her sister Layla was buying her own spread with her fiancé, Joshua Banks. Like them, Chelsea could strike out on her own.

Or she could start a business like her youngest sister. Morgan owned a successful fashion boutique in town called the Rancher's Daughter. Chelsea suspected that her sister had realized early on that with three older siblings managing the ranch, there wouldn't be room for her. The feisty redhead seemed perfectly happy doing her own thing. Could Chelsea find joy being anywhere but here?

She angled toward her bedroom, hoping a shower would clear her head and revive her flagging energy. She had a full day of celebrations ahead of her. The whole family was attending the town's annual Fourth of July parade and picnic. Later, they would head to the Texas Cattleman's Club. Every year the club hosted a barbecue and fireworks to celebrate the holiday.

As she reached the hallway that led to her bedroom, she spied her mother coming down the hall toward her.

"I was just looking for you." Bethany Grandin made no attempt to hide her disappointment as she surveyed her daughter's disheveled appearance. "Oh, you're not ready to go."

"I just got back from…" She trailed off, seeing her mother wasn't really listening. Bethany shared her husband's resistance to their daughters working the ranch. Chelsea had long ago learned to just do things and stop explaining herself.

Bethany glanced at the gold watch on her wrist.

Diamonds sparkled on the twenty-fifth wedding anniversary present from her husband. "The parade starts in an hour."

"I know. It won't take me long to shower and change." Chelsea eased past her mother. A garment bag lay on her bed. "What's that?"

"Just a little something from your sister's boutique that I thought would work for today." Bethany adored shopping and often bought things for her children to wear.

Clearly her mother believed that Chelsea was neglecting her appearance. And maybe Bethany was right. As much as Chelsea enjoyed dressing up, lately, when left to her own devices, she wore jeans, boots and whatever shirt came to hand.

"That's really nice of you."

Bethany seemed to relax at her daughter's response. No doubt she'd been expecting a battle. Chelsea sighed. Was she really that prickly and difficult to deal with? She didn't want to be. She just wanted to be appreciated for who she was, not ignored or changed into somebody else's vision of her.

"I saw it at Morgan's boutique, and I immediately thought of you." Her mother unzipped the garment bag and pulled out a red halter dress with a full skirt.

"Wow." The obligatory smile she'd pasted onto her lips turned into an oh of appreciation as Chelsea pictured how great the bold color would look against her dark hair and brown eyes.

"And there's lipstick to match." Bethany scooped up a gold tube from Chelsea's nightstand. "I looked all over until I found the perfect shade to go with the dress."

Chelsea took the lipstick and opened it. The bright red color triggered her anxiety. She was not the family beauty. Layla and Morgan were the ones who'd inherited their mother's delicate features and fair coloring, while Chelsea and Vic favored their father, with dark brown hair and eyes. But where Victor John's strong bone structure and eyebrows made her brother handsome, their boldness left Chelsea feeling far from dainty and feminine.

"I know it's not something you would've chosen," her mother said, fondling the soft material. "But you have the perfect figure for this dress, and I thought you might like it."

Translation: *it would be nice if you went back to dressing like a girl again.* Chelsea knew her mother was right. She just hated falling short when compared to her beautiful, stylish sisters.

"It's very nice." And she would definitely get noticed wearing the dress. Unfortunately, it wasn't the type of recognition she craved. Chelsea briefly wallowed in regret. She wanted to stand out for her achievements, not her appearance. "But is it a bit too much for a parade and TCC barbecue?"

"Too much?" Bethany's face fell, and Chelsea silently cursed.

"You have such wonderful taste." Seeing her mother was only partially mollified by the compliment, Chelsea cast about for a way to distract her further. "In fact, I was thinking that maybe you could help me with something else."

"Of course I'll help. What did you have in mind?"

Spying the outdated Paris-themed wallpaper and matching decor in her room, Chelsea latched on to an idea. Little had changed since she'd gone off to college seventeen years earlier. At the time she'd been obsessed with Paris and even considered spending a year studying overseas, but in the end, she'd decided to be more practical and selected an agriculture major that made sense for a future rancher.

Now the room was a vivid reminder of paths not taken. Perhaps it was time to erase this reminder of the possibilities she'd once embraced. Time to forget that her dreams had involved something besides running Grandin Ranch. She just needed to redouble her focus and convince her father to listen to all her ideas to improve the ranch.

If he heard her out, he'd see the value in instituting new pasture rotation techniques to maximize the quality of the grass their herd fed on and agree to incorporate new bloodlines to strengthen the quality of their stock. Already she'd implemented a number of technology-based applications that allowed her to monitor the health of the cattle.

"I was just thinking that maybe I should do something with my room. It could use a makeover." Seeing her mother's eyes begin to glow with excitement, Chelsea impulsively rushed on. "I honestly don't know what I would do in here. And you are so good at decorating."

"Oh, that's a wonderful idea. I've been dying to renovate this room for a while now." Bethany didn't add that Chelsea's room was the last one in the ranch house lacking her mother's creative flair. In fact, many rooms had been through two or even three renovations.

Chelsea winced at her mother's obvious enthusiasm. "I guess it's a little bit like a time capsule in here."

"A bit." Her mother gave a relieved laugh before enfolding her daughter in a spirited hug. "I'll leave you to get ready. Do you want us to wait for you?"

"I'll drive myself." If she took her time making herself presentable, Chelsea didn't want to hold any of them up.

Bethany looked worried. "You are planning to come?"

"Yes, I promise I'll be there." She pumped extra cheer into her tone to be convincing. "Wearing that." She indicated the dress and then held up the lipstick. "And this."

"You're going to look fantastic."

Her mother's prophecy turned out to be closer to fact than Chelsea expected, which was confirmed by her best friend as the two women rendezvoused on Main Street to watch the parade.

"Girl, you look amazing." This was quite a compliment coming from Natalie Hastings, who had a stylish wardrobe that would be the envy of the pickiest fashionistas. "Where has this Chelsea been hiding these last two years?"

Tall and curvy with long, dark hair and flawless tawny-brown skin, Natalie shared Chelsea's ambition when it came to her career, but she hadn't abandoned her personal life entirely. It was just that the younger woman had an unrequited crush on the elusive Jonathan Lattimore, Chelsea's neighbor. But if Natalie lacked confidence when it came to love, she was always on the prowl for her friend.

"Hey."

The parade had been underway for half an hour, and Chelsea had let her thoughts drift back to the ranch and what it would take to convince her father that she—and not Vic—should take over running things when he retired.

"Ouch." Chelsea hadn't responded to her best friend fast enough and received an elbow nudged into her ribs. Scowling, she shot Natalie a frown and found her friend's attention wasn't on the parade. "What?"

"Don't look now, but Nolan Thurston has been staring at you for the last ten minutes."

"Nolan Thurston?" Icy dismay raised goose bumps on her arm. "Are you sure?" Chelsea was glad her gaze was hidden behind designer sunglasses as she scanned the crowd across the street. "I don't see him."

"He's standing in front of Royal Gents."

A float interrupted her view, and Chelsea shook her head. "I'm sure it's nothing. Or maybe it's because of what's going on between our families."

Nolan had returned to Royal right around the time Chelsea's grandfather had died and had joined his brother, Heath, in making the Grandin family's lives hell. Nolan and Heath had produced documents claiming their mother, Cynthia Thurston, owned the oil rights beneath the ranches belonging to the Grandin family and their neighbors the Lattimores.

"I don't know. It was more like a sexy stare." Natalie's lips pursed. "Like he saw something he liked and wants to get it naked."

Natalie's assessment was a bottle rocket zipping straight at Chelsea's head. Adrenaline shot through her, prompting a shocked laugh.

"That's nuts."

Although she'd seen Nolan around town and at the Texas Cattleman's Club, they'd never once spoken. She'd gone out of her way to avoid both the Thurston brothers, not wanting to vent her wrath at whatever they were up to and get into a public argument.

"Is it?" Natalie sounded wistful.

"Layla is more his type." Once again Chelsea was searching through a gap in the parade for Nolan. "He hit on her when he first came to town."

"Because he wanted information about your family. Not because he was interested in her."

The mysterious granting of the oil rights by Chelsea's grandfather had shaken all parties. At first the Grandin family had suspected the whole thing had been a huge scam perpetrated by the Thurston twins, but soon it became apparent that Chelsea's uncle David had actually had an affair with Cynthia around the time she'd gotten pregnant with her daughter, Ashley. Mysteriously, the document hadn't come to light until after mother and daughter had died in an accident. Now Heath Thurston, in concert with his twin, was determined to grow their wealth at the expense of the Grandin and Lattimore ranches.

"Maybe since he struck out with Layla, he's coming for me next?" Chelsea proposed.

"You know, there's another possibility…"

"Such as?"

As she asked the question, her gaze found the dark-haired twins standing on the opposite side of the parade route. Even with the width of the downtown Royal street between them, she could tell that Nolan was indeed staring at her. Something dangerous and exciting lit up her nerve endings. Strangely short of breath, Chelsea barely registered Natalie's answer.

"It's possible he didn't recognize you all gussied up like this. We've been best friends forever, and I almost walked past you earlier."

Chelsea didn't think she'd deliberately downplayed her femininity because of her father's unfair prejudice against her gender, but for the last few years, she'd ignored her closet full of dresses in favor of strutting around town in jeans and cowboy boots. It was foolish to think by dressing like a guy that her father would see her as a capable rancher first and his eldest daughter second.

"Maybe he's just a gorgeous guy interested in a sexy gal." Natalie's gaze bounced from Nolan Thurston to Chelsea. "With his yummy dark eyes and those bold eyebrows, combined with your fantastic bone structure, you two would make beautiful babies."

Chelsea was a second too slow to stop the bark of

shocked laughter that burst from her. "Oh, jeez." She rolled her eyes dismissively while her stomach did a disconcerting somersault. "Whatever. I don't have time for anything having to do with Nolan Thurston and his luscious bedroom eyes."

"Not even if it meant getting a leg up on your brother?"

"I'm listening." Chelsea brought her full attention to bear on her best friend.

"What's the biggest crisis on the ranch right now?"

"The oil rights claim."

Natalie nodded sagely. "So Nolan offered to take Layla to lunch to 'talk things out.' But obviously Layla knew he just wanted to get information. What if you turn the tables on him and do the same thing to him? If you save the ranch by stopping the oil rights claim, your dad would have no choice but to put you in charge."

Most of the time she used straightforward tactics to try to beat out her brother for control of the ranch. She wanted to win through hard work and good judgment. But sexism cloaked in tradition was alive and well in her family. And thinking about it now, Chelsea reckoned if she didn't give it everything she had, maybe she didn't deserve to be in charge.

Resolve blazed inside Chelsea. "I like the way you think."

Whatever it took to beat Vic. That was what she'd promised herself.

Her gaze flicked toward the Thurston twins and skimmed over Nolan. A little weakness invaded her knees as she thought about what dating him might entail. One thing was for certain—spending time with such a handsome man would be equal parts pleasure and satisfaction.

And in the end, she'd save her ranch.

Maybe it was about time that being female became an asset.

Chelsea linked arms with her friend. "How do I go about casually bumping into Nolan Thurston?"

The heat that consumed Nolan Thurston had nothing to do with the ninety-four-degree temperature radiating from the pavement or the confining press of the parade crowd around him. No, the cause of the inferno was that the sizzling brunette in the sexy red dress had finally noticed him. Damn, the woman was striking. He liked his women tall, lithe, but with curves in all the right places, and she looked to be the perfect blend of all that. Her dark brown hair fell in sexy waves over her delicate shoulders, and he imagined himself twining the silky locks around his wrists as he pulled her in for a hot, deep kiss.

When was the last time he'd gazed at a woman and felt something hit him like a brick wall? A long, long time. A float interrupted his view of the woman who'd sparked his interest, and it was as if a cloud had passed in front of the sun. Suddenly Nolan was desperate—he had to get across the street before she vanished. He simply had to get up close and personal to see if she was as bewitching in person.

As Nolan began to edge his way forward, a hand caught his arm. "Hey! Where are you going?"

Nolan glanced over his shoulder at his brother. Being apart from Heath for fifteen years had made him forget what it was like to look at his twin and feel that crazy disorientation of seeing himself reflected in another's features. It was a little like looking in the mirror but not recognizing yourself.

Heath had always been the more serious and responsible brother. These days the somber stranger with the weight of the world on his shoulders bore no resemblance to the mischievous twin of old. The brothers might share the same features, but they each wore the years differently.

"There's a woman I'm dying to get to know." Nolan indicated the opposite side of the street, where the lady in red stood.

A grin transformed Heath's features, making him much more approachable. "Who?"

"That's what I'd like to find out."

Between the two of them, Nolan was the flirt, the one women flocked to because of his easy charm and daring ways. Heath's more serious demeanor didn't scare away the ladies—his handsome features and rugged physique always attracted attention—but he wasn't usually focused on romance.

"Which one is she?" Heath eyed the crowd opposite them as if he might be able to guess his brother's taste in women.

"The one in the red dress across the way." Even as he spoke, the trailing edge of the float moved by and revealed her once more. A bottled-up sigh slipped free. Absolutely stunning.

"Let's see. A red dress, you say… Whoa!" Heath gave his head a vigorous shake. "You definitely cannot go there."

"Why?" Nolan felt his insides clench at his brother's emphatic declaration. "Did you date her?"

"Did I date…?" Heath gaped at him. "Don't you know who that is?"

Nolan was utterly confused. "Should I?"

"That's Chelsea *Grandin*."

Hearing the emphasis his brother put on the last name, Nolan narrowed his eyes and inspected her once more. "Are you sure? That looks nothing like Chelsea." Where was the no-nonsense rancher's daughter in sensible denim and boots? This vision in red had wayward, touchable hair, big brown eyes and glorious, full red lips. "She's a knockout."

"I'm sure." Heath's statement sounded like the fall of a judge's gavel. The decision was final. Nolan could have nothing to do with anyone in the Grandin family.

Two months ago, he'd been stunned when Heath explained about the document he'd found among their mother's things granting her rights to the oil beneath the Grandin and Lattimore ranches. And when Heath had asked him to come to Royal, Texas, to help him make the claim, of course he'd said yes. The brothers had not been on the best terms even before Nolan left town at eighteen. Nolan was hoping to repair that.

While Heath had always felt connected to their

family's ranch and worked hard not just to keep it going, but to make it thrive, Nolan had a completely different passion. Unconcerned by money or the need to hold tight to things, he'd packed up his limited possessions, slung a backpack over his shoulder and headed west. A few weeks later, he'd landed in Los Angeles.

For many young hopefuls, Tinseltown was the end of the journey, but for Nolan, it was only the beginning. Within a week, he'd connected with a guy looking for crew to help him deliver a yacht to Singapore. With the experience he gained during that voyage, Nolan then spent the next three years working a series of private yachts doing charters. It was during one of these voyages in the Mediterranean that he'd met wealthy studio executive Skip McGrath and embarked on a career in reality TV production. Scouting filming locations gave him the opportunity to work in any number of exotic areas. Seeing the world had been his dream since he was a kid, and making a living while doing so was absolutely perfect.

The only dark spot in an otherwise idyllic life was his estrangement with his twin. The only time in fifteen years that Nolan had returned to Royal was to attend the double funeral of his mother and sister two years earlier. He'd been worried how Heath would react to seeing him again, but grief had provided a bridge for the brothers to reconcile. Since then, their relationship had improved somewhat. The shocking loss had sparked their communication, and they'd spoken more often, but they had a long way to go.

Which was part of what had spurred Nolan to return to Royal. He hoped that a shared goal would reignite the close bond they'd enjoyed as kids, but Heath's obsession with getting the full value of what was theirs left him prickly, and Nolan couldn't seem to gain his brother's trust.

That his mission was going to stir up the town and compel their friends and neighbors to pick sides didn't seem to worry Heath at all. Small-town living wasn't for everyone, and all the reasons Nolan had put Royal behind him came rushing back. Even though Royal was an affluent town with sprawling ranches, high-end shopping and luxury hotels, Nolan had felt confined by the community. Maybe it was how everyone knew what was going on with their neighbors, or the way his family was tied to the land they owned.

Nolan had been obsessed with getting beyond the city limits and seeing what the world had to offer. He'd been lucky that a series of opportunities had landed him in Skip's orbit and led to Nolan traveling to some amazing parts of the world—as well as some seriously sketchy locales and rough terrain. He'd loved every dangerous, uncomfortable, eye-opening moment of his years spent adventuring. But the cost of living his dream was losing the brother he loved.

"You really think she's attractive?" Heath's thoughtful murmur caught Nolan off guard.

"Yeah. Of course." He glanced toward the attractive brunette only to realize that she'd disappeared. His mood dipped. "Don't you?"

Heath shrugged. "I've never really thought about it."

"If I recall, you were always more attracted to blondes." Nolan thought about his own failed attempt to cozy up to Layla Grandin in an effort to gain some insight into why their mother, Cynthia, had had a document granting her rights to the oil beneath the Grandin ranch. "Maybe you're the one who should've taken a crack at Layla. She's pretty enough, but my heart wasn't really in it. I think that's why I asked Layla to bring Chelsea along, but I had no idea Chelsea could look like that."

As sexy as he found beautiful, confident women, when he'd seen Chelsea around town, she'd hidden her expression beneath the brim of a Stetson, and he realized that he'd seen more of her backside heading in the opposite direction.

Confronted by this new insight, Nolan frowned. Could she have been avoiding him? Given the conflict between their families, it would make sense that she might not wish to have anything to do with him. His senses tingled in anticipation of a chase.

"What if I get to know Chelsea a bit?" Nolan proposed, glancing toward his twin. "I might have better luck connecting with her than I did with her sister."

"This isn't a good idea." But Heath wasn't as emphatic as he'd been earlier.

"Look, I can do this. Half my job is negotiating."

"Just remember, don't give up more information than you get."

Since he had very little knowledge about his brother's strategy or motivation, that wasn't going to be a problem. And maybe if he found out something that would help their cause, Heath would start treating him like his twin again instead of keeping Nolan at arm's length.

"I've had dinner with billionaires in Istanbul, spent weeks living in the jungle while hunting for the perfect location in Indonesia and been confronted by crocodiles in Australia. I'm lucky, resourceful and persistent."

"Chelsea is smart and will see you coming from a mile away."

Nolan shrugged. Why waste time touting his skills when he could let his success speak for itself? "No harm in taking a swing."

"You'll strike out."

"It's a chance worth taking. And you never know—" Nolan shot his brother a cocky grin. "She might have a taste for adventure."

Heath snorted. "I doubt that."

"Challenge accepted," Nolan crowed, mentally rubbing his hands together.

Two

Nolan hadn't imagined a knockout in a red dress would all be that hard to spot, but he hadn't taken into account that most of the town would be wearing an assortment of red, white and blue clothing. Still, after coming up empty after half an hour of searching, Nolan was starting to worry that she'd already left. Disappointment hit. He hadn't realized how much he'd been looking forward to encountering Chelsea Grandin until his hopes had been dashed.

Hoping he'd have better luck at the barbecue, Nolan headed for the Texas Cattleman's Club. On the drive, he realized a lot of women had passed through his life, some more memorable than others. He wasn't accustomed to pursuing any of them with anywhere near the enthusiasm that drove him to search through the barbecue attendees. Nolan acknowledged that he had a mission. They needed information—or, better yet, an ally. He also recognized that he'd keyed into her before discovering that she was a Grandin.

Someone bumped into his back. The impact jarred him out of his thoughts. Given the crush of people milling about the gardens, he wasn't surprised by the contact.

"Oh, sorry," came a husky female voice.

Nolan caught a whiff of passion fruit and was transported to Brazil. He'd spent nearly a month in the southern end of the country, scouting a location near Iguazu Falls. The scent of wild passion fruit had hung heavy in the air as macaws had flown through the dense canopy above his head. He pivoted to face the woman who'd run into him.

Chelsea Grandin.

His heart did a crazy jig at his first glimpse of her large brown eyes, soft with apology. Although he'd been searching high and low for her, Nolan hadn't been prepared for the lightning that went through him at suddenly finding her within arm's reach. A smudge of sauce near her mouth drew his attention to her ruby-red lips. Shocked by the urge to bend down and lick the barbecue sauce from her skin, Nolan backed up half a step.

"It was all my fault," Nolan responded, a little short of breath. An irrepressible smile twitched at his lips as he noticed a dimple appearing in her cheek at his suave counter.

"Not true. You were standing still. It was entirely me. I think I stepped in a hole."

Nolan's gaze followed hers as she glanced down at the ground near her feet. Given the fancy dress she wore, he expected her to be in high-heeled sandals. Instead, she wore a sensible pair of cowboy boots in cognac leather, inset with white stars.

"I just lost my balance for a second." Her enormous eyes went impossibly wide. "Oh, I didn't get any barbecue sauce on you, I hope."

Before he could assure her he didn't care if she had, she slipped around him, her fingers trailing over his shirt as she checked for damage. Nolan stood frozen while a thousand nerve endings blazed beneath her light touch.

"Oh, good," she declared on a relieved sigh. "Looks like we dodged a bullet."

Had he?

His clothes might have been all right, but the hit to his equilibrium rocked him. Thunder rumbled through his muscles as she completed her inspection and returned to stand before him.

"I'm Nolan."

For some reason he'd left off his last name. Maybe given his immediate, intense physical reaction to her, he was reluctant to see her open expression slam closed when she realized he was a Thurston. Yet he and Heath were twins. He scoured her expression for some sign of recognition. When he glimpsed neither caution nor hostility, he grew suspicious. His brother had overset her entire family by pursuing a claim for the oil rights beneath her land. Why wasn't she treating him like the enemy?

"Chelsea." Her wide lips curved in a genuine smile, further confusing him.

After making sure her right hand was free of barbecue, she held it out to him. The rough calluses on the palm that connected with his affirmed that this wasn't a woman who sat back and let others do the work. His interest in her flared still brighter, making him regret the animosity between their families.

"I've seen you around town," he said, dipping his toe into the murky situation. "But never dressed like this." He let his appreciation shine as he flicked his gaze along her slim form. "You look like a firecracker ready to explode."

Her husky chuckle raised goose bumps on his arms. The bold interest lighting her eyes twisted up his insides. Lust at first sight wasn't an unfamiliar phenomenon to him, but few women presented the sort of intriguing danger Chelsea Grandin embodied.

Heath's warning filled his thoughts. Nolan wished he understood his brother's obsession, but Heath hadn't been all that forthcoming with explanations, and Nolan hadn't wanted to rock the boat by demanding answers. When Heath trusted him, Nolan would get clarity. Until then, he'd support his brother and hope that when he'd proved his loyalty, Heath would confide in him.

"It's hot enough that I just might." She sent him a

smoky look from beneath her lashes before indicating a nearby booth. "Feel like buying a girl a glass of lemonade?"

"Sure."

Without a backward glance to see if he was following, she headed off. Obviously, she was confident he wouldn't let her get away. Nolan hesitated a brief moment, just long enough to admire the way her hips flared out from the indent of her tiny waist. Loath to lose her in the crowded garden, he shot after her, neatly navigating between two converging groups to reach her side.

At the lemonade stand, he exchanged a bill for two paper cups adorned with lemons.

As they moved away, Chelsea scanned the nearby picnic tables. "Let's find a place to sit down?"

"How about there?" He indicated a narrow space that they could both just squeeze into.

She eyed his selection and then gave an approving nod. He waited for her to settle before joining her. Although he was firmly sandwiched between her and a beefy cowboy, Nolan only noticed the soft, feminine body pressed against his left side.

"Here," she said, nudging the plate his way. "Have some of these. It's way too much for me to eat all by myself."

He considered refusing, but as the scent of the fragrant barbecue reached his nose, his stomach picked that moment to growl. "I am a little hungry." A pause. "I could go get my own…"

Even as he offered, he hoped she'd repeat her invitation to share. He was afraid she'd disappear again if he left her even briefly. What if someone approached her while he was gone and filled her ear with warnings?

To his relief, Chelsea shook her head.

"Help me finish these first."

"Sure."

The meal that followed went into his memory as one of the most delicious, carnal events he'd experienced. Not only were the ribs tender and perfectly smoked, but watching Chelsea's even white teeth tear the meat off the bone made the July day even hotter.

"What do you think of Royal's Fourth of July celebration?" Chelsea asked when there was nothing left of the feast but a pile of bones. "Did you enjoy the parade?"

"To be honest, I wasn't paying attention."

"Too small-town?" she teased.

Nolan shook his head. "Too distracted."

"Oh?"

At one point during the parade, he'd been certain that she'd noticed his interest, but since she'd been so far away and wearing sunglasses, he couldn't say for sure. Equally mystifying was the way she was acting as if she had no idea who he was.

While the oil rights claim that had put their families into conflict loomed large in his thoughts, he hesitated to bring the matter up. If she didn't mention the elephant in the room, he wasn't going to. Maybe she,

too, wanted to explore the attraction between them—
or could it be that she was planning on pumping him
for information?

"There was a certain woman across the way who
caught my eye, and I couldn't seem to look away."

"Can you describe her? Maybe I know who she is."

Was this one big flirtation, or was she as ingenu-
ous as she appeared? As a tactic, it was working. The
uncertainty had thrown off his rhythm.

"Long brown hair. Scorching-hot red dress. Kiss-
able red lips. She blew my mind."

"From thirty feet away?" Chelsea blinked in surprise. Color had bloomed in her cheeks at his description. "Wow! She must have made quite an impression."

He set his elbow on the table and dropped his chin
into his palm. With his gaze resting on her, Nolan
said, "She was a total knockout."

"So, if you found this woman, what would you
want to do with her?"

She was testing him, trying to decide what sort of
man he was. Nolan realized that, for all her banter,
Chelsea Grandin was cautious, guarded and maybe
even controlling. In many ways she reminded him
of Heath. Although his twin wasn't firstborn—their
sister, Ashley, had been five years older—but Heath
had been the firstborn boy, and where Nolan had been
outgoing and self-centered, Heath had shouldered responsibility without complaint."

"I'd like to get to know her better." A shiver stole
down his spine as her red lips curved into a crooked
smile.

"And if she's already spoken for?"

Her counter caught him off guard. Was Chelsea dating someone? Heath hadn't mentioned a boyfriend, but then, his brother's singular focus kept him from visualizing the big picture.

"Obviously if she's married, it's my loss. But any other relationship status I consider fair game."

"You're pretty sure of your appeal. What do you bring to the table that might interest her?"

Damn. This woman was making him work. Not that he was afraid of a challenge. He'd tackled the Bhutan Snowman Trek, a twenty-five-day journey over eleven passes of forty-five hundred meters in elevation that defined the border between Tibet and Bhutan. He'd trained for six months before attempting it.

"Adventure. Excitement. Romance."

With each word he spoke, eager curiosity grew in her soft brown eyes.

"Hmm," she murmured. "Sounds nice."

Convinced he was taking the right tack, Nolan stroked a strand of hair off her cheek and slid it behind her ear. "What do you say, Chelsea? Are you game?"

Chelsea found herself shockingly short of breath beneath Nolan's intense regard. Was she game? Hell, yes. Maybe too game? She'd need to watch herself with this one. Even without the troubles between their families, he was not the sort she'd usually choose to go out with.

The men she preferred to date were structured and

predictable. From the moment she'd met him, she'd decided Nolan Thurston was going to be anything but.

"What did you have in mind?"

"Dinner?" His eyebrows rose. "Unless you'd like to try something more adventurous."

Excitement ignited at his dare, sparking her uneasiness. Chelsea had never met anyone as intriguing as Nolan. Which probably explained why, since seeing him at the parade, she'd avoided thinking about the ranch and the problems filling up her bucket of woes. Now she reveled in his engaging grin and come-hither dark brown eyes. With his solid, muscular body pressed against hers in the narrow space, she had a hard time keeping her wits about her.

She took a second to remind herself that spending time with him was a means to an end. She'd approached him because of the oil rights claim against her family's land. Still, there was no reason she couldn't enjoy herself while convincing him that pursuing their claim wouldn't be worth their while. A successful outcome for her family would demonstrate once and for all that the Grandin Ranch should be hers to run.

Chelsea shook herself free of his spell. "Let's start with dinner and see how it goes."

"Wonderful. Are you free this week?"

"I'm available Tuesday or Thursday." She didn't want him to think that her social schedule was wide-open, and a weeknight was more casual for a first date than a weekend. Plus, to keep him wanting more, she could always cut the date short, claiming that she started her mornings early. Which she did.

"Tuesday, then. I don't want to wait any longer than I have to." His wolfish smile curled her toes.

Did he really not know she was a Grandin? Granted, they hadn't exchanged last names, but he'd been standing next to his brother at the parade, and Heath knew exactly who she was. The fact that neither one of them had acknowledged their connection or brought up the oil rights claim reminded her to be wary of trickery.

They exchanged phone numbers, but neither made any move to part. Instead, they stood smiling at each other like a couple of smitten teenagers while the sounds emanating from the crowded garden faded to white noise.

"This has been fun." Chelsea heard equal notes of pleasure and reluctance in her voice as she attempted to extricate herself from Nolan.

Sharing the plate of barbecue with him had proved as distracting as it had been delightful. What it hadn't been was productive. Neither one of them had acknowledged the connection between their families.

"A lot of fun," Nolan agreed, pinning her with a smoky gaze. "I can't recall a meal I enjoyed more."

Chelsea told her feet to move, but none of her mental goading convinced her muscles to function. She'd gotten him to bite, now she just needed to set the hook. That meant walking away. *Leave him wanting more.*

"We could get dessert," she suggested instead, cursing her craving for more time with him.

"It is a hot day." His gaze glanced off her lips, making her shiver. "Ice cream back in town?"

"Perfect." The drive should give her time to start thinking straight.

He dropped the remains of their shared barbecue into nearest trash receptacle. She gave him directions to her favorite ice-cream shop on Main Street and told him she'd meet him there.

In the shop's cool interior, Chelsea breathed in the vanilla scent of freshly made waffle cones mingling with the rich aroma of hot fudge. They each chose their favorite flavor—Nolan surprised her by choosing cookie dough.

With the sweet taste of chocolate melting on her tongue, Chelsea and Nolan meandered along the shady side of Main Street where the parade had passed several hours earlier and settled on a bench outside the bank. While Nolan half lounged with his long legs stretched out before him, one arm draped over the back of the bench behind her, Chelsea perched on the edge, knees primly locked together, and surreptitiously peeked at his magnificent physique.

Having no idea what to say, she couldn't believe it when she blurted out the first thing that came to mind. "What is your favorite color?" She quickly used her tongue to chase a drip running down the side of her cone to hide her embarrassment.

When Nolan didn't immediately reply to her question, she glanced over and caught him watching her with intense fascination. Something sexy and primal vibrated behind her belly button as she imagined gliding her tongue along his skin in a similar fashion.

"Red. I spotted you across the road and couldn't take my eyes off you." His voice dipped into husky undertones as if he truly meant what he said.

"Oh." Chelsea was at a loss. Despite knowing that he was trouble, he seemed so damned genuine, and she wanted to be swayed by his openness. In fact, several times over the last hour, she'd lost track of the real reason she'd approached him in the first place. "Are you always this direct?"

"Usually. When I see something and immediately know in my gut that it's right, I tend to be single-minded and straightforward."

Should she infer that she was that something right for him? It was flattering to think a glimpse of her from so far away could have caused such conviction in him, but maybe that's exactly what he intended for her to think. Hadn't their connection formed a little too smoothly? He had to know who she was. After all, he'd been in town for a couple months. Heath would've pointed out the entire Grandin clan to Nolan. This sudden burst of insight triggered Chelsea's guards. And just in time. She had been on the brink of believing all his romantic chitchat.

Recalled to the dangerous nature of her mission, Chelsea reviewed their conversation. What tidbit of information had she let slip that might've given Nolan something he could take back to his brother? Nothing came to mind. But she'd been pretty swept away by his charm.

He'd proven to be far more charming and interesting than she'd expected. Chelsea was no longer confident in her ability to manipulate Nolan.

The Texas heat prevented Chelsea from lingering over her ice-cream cone. The frozen treat was melting fast, and she had to gulp it down before the sticky mess dripped all over her. As she popped the last bit of sugary cone into her mouth, she decided it was a blessing in disguise. If she delayed her exit much longer, he might get the idea that she was smitten.

"This has been fun, but my family is probably wondering where I got off to," Chelsea said, getting to her feet. "I guess I'll see you on Tuesday."

"No guesswork needed." Nolan's slow smile made her vibrate with anticipation. "You definitely will."

Chelsea made no effort to hide her delight as she flashed him an answering grin. Playing games wasn't her forte. That being said, it was exactly what she'd committed to doing with Nolan. Still, if she hadn't found him attractive, she'd never have been able to flirt with him in a genuine way.

She'd walked a block before realizing that she'd headed in the opposite direction from where she'd parked her car. Cursing her addled brain, she traveled another half block to her sister's boutique and ducked into the Rancher's Daughter. The tinkling bell over the door notified the salesclerk that someone had entered the shop. Kerri looked up from the accessories she was unpacking and smiled when she caught sight of Chelsea.

"Is Morgan around today?" Chelsea indicated the dress she was wearing. "I just wanted to show her the dress Mom bought for me here."

"She's in the back." Kerri's attention returned to the necklaces she'd been pulling from their plastic wrapping.

Chelsea found the youngest Grandin sibling in her small office at the back of the store. Morgan was perusing an online catalog of dresses and jotting notes on a legal pad beside her keyboard.

"Working on a holiday?" Chelsea asked from the doorway.

With seven years and two siblings between them, Chelsea and Morgan had never formed the tight bond that Chelsea shared with Layla. It didn't help their relationship that Morgan sided with Vic all the time. Not only was he her older brother, but they were close in age, and as such the pair was thick as thieves. So it wasn't a surprise that when it came to the debate on who should be in charge of Grandin Ranch, Morgan thought her brother was the right choice.

"I've got a few things I wanted to check on before heading to the Texas Cattleman's Club for the fireworks." Morgan sized up her sister's ensemble and nodded in approval. "The boots are a surprising choice, but they work. You should really dress up more often."

Chelsea thought about her upcoming date with Nolan and decided she would buy something sexy and sophisticated to boost her confidence. "You're right. I'm going to take a look around and see if anything catches my eye."

When Morgan nodded absently and returned to work, Chelsea headed back into the shop. Buzzing with anticipation, she selected several dresses and went to try them on. Once again, she marveled at her sister's fashion sense as she narrowed her choices down to three. After much deliberating, she couldn't settle on which one to buy. It wasn't like her to dither when making decisions. Of course, lately all her decisions had been to benefit the ranch. There, she could weigh the pros and cons of various strategies and formulate the best solution.

This was different. She was trying to create an emotional reaction in someone she didn't know at all. What would appeal to Nolan? Did she hit him with something flirty and romantic or drop-dead sexy? Did she want to win his heart or scramble his brains with lust? The latter seemed far easier and less emotionally treacherous.

As the full impact of what she was doing struck her, Chelsea sat down in the dressing room. What had seemed like a perfectly sensible scheme when Natalie proposed it was quickly becoming complicated. Was she really considering hooking up with Nolan under false pretenses? She was both excited and horrified at her daring, but the potential to save the ranch and win her father's approval was hard to ignore.

She balled her fists in her lap and told her racing heart to chill. There was a lot at stake, both for her and the ranch. She'd never balked at high stakes before. Why start now? As long as she kept her own emotions under control and her eye on the prize, nothing would go wrong.

Three

After parting from Chelsea, Nolan headed to his rental. The thousand-square-foot converted loft in a former furniture store off First Avenue was similar to his place in downtown LA and more familiar than the ranch house he'd grown up in. He'd been worried that living with Heath would bring up too many uncomfortable memories. Sharing tight quarters with people for extended periods of time could be stressful—a little something he'd learned while crewing on a luxury yacht for nearly a year.

Unfortunately, he'd forgotten this lesson three years ago when he'd agreed to produce a documentary about a research vessel studying whale migration near the South Pole. Four months of flaring tempers and personality conflicts had reminded Nolan why he preferred to travel solo.

No doubt most people would find his lifestyle lonely and undesirable, but Nolan liked the freedom to do as he chose. He wasn't used to having his comings and goings tracked, and even though he wasn't living on Thurston Ranch, Heath was keeping close tabs on him. Maybe his brother was worried that Nolan would vanish into the night again. Whatever Heath's concerns, Nolan was finding that being back in Royal was proving to be more of an adjustment than he'd expected.

It brought up the same urge to hit the trail as when he was eighteen. Back then Royal had felt small and confining despite its proximity to Dallas. Looking back, however, Nolan thought his discomfort had been less about the town and more about everyone's expectations. Not that he'd felt pressure to take over the ranch. Heath had stepped into their father's shoes after he died, but having to decide about college and a career had made Nolan feel constrained. The last thing he'd wanted was to be tied down.

His phone chimed to indicate an incoming text as he shut and locked the front door behind him. As he dropped his keys onto the counter, Nolan wondered if he was heading back to LA. He was waiting to hear about several reality show projects that would soon need him to scout locations. If the studios were ready to head into development, Nolan would have to decide if he should turn down the lucrative work and stay in Royal to help Heath, or leave his brother to fend for himself.

Passing on the scouting jobs could mean the executive producers would be less likely to reach out to him later. He needed to figure out how long he expected to stay in Royal. He was on a month-to-month lease with this loft, so he could pick up and go at any time. Of course, it was also a risk to abandon his brother to battle the oil rights claim alone against the Lattimores and Grandins. This might set their relationship back to square one.

To Nolan's relief, Heath was the one reaching out. He wouldn't have to make a lose-lose decision today.

How'd it go with Chelsea Grandin?

Although the question was straightforward, Heath's tension came through loud and clear. Nolan's twin had been consumed by the oil rights for reasons he hadn't made clear. It wasn't that Heath needed the money. The ranch was doing well, even better than it had been when Nolan left. He wished his brother would confide what was really going on. Not that he blamed Heath for his reticence. It wasn't like the twins had communicated in the years since Nolan's precipitous exit from Royal at eighteen.

I have a date with her Tuesday night. Any idea where I should take her?

Below his text message, a trio of blinking dots indicated his brother was typing a message. Nolan watched it for several seconds, anticipating a reply. When none came and the seconds ticked by, he set the phone down and went to grab a beer from the refrigerator. By the time he picked up his phone once more, there were no dots and no message.

Nolan was about ready to give up and do his own research when his phone lit up with a call.

"Tell me everything she said," Heath demanded without preliminaries.

"I don't know that I remember everything," Nolan hedged, suspecting Heath wouldn't appreciate how much energy Nolan had expended flirting with Chelsea and that they'd not discussed the oil rights or even mentioned that their families were connected.

"Well, what do you remember?"

Nolan sighed. Sometimes Heath was too direct. Could he convince his brother that an investigation into her family history was going to take time and finesse? And maybe even a little seduction.

"We didn't talk about the document you found, and I didn't bring up our shared family history." Nolan paused for a second, hearing his brother's heavy exhalation. "Look, I need to gain her trust, and that's not going to happen over a plate of ribs."

"I get it." Heath sounded resigned—unsurprised. "Thanks for trying."

That his brother was already throwing in the towel made Nolan grind his teeth. It was just like Heath to dismiss Nolan's abilities. He was one of the most sought-after location scouts in the industry and a stellar negotiator, but Heath only saw his twin as his younger brother.

As a kid, Heath had never hesitated to voice his strong opinions and bully his twin if Nolan's ideas differed. Several times in the last couple months, Heath had offhandedly disparaged what Nolan did, not understanding how his twin could make a good living while getting to do something he loved.

"Oh, I'm not done," Nolan said, growing all the more determined. "I fully intend to figure out everything Chelsea knows. That way we can establish a strategy for winning the legal battles that are sure to be waged against your claim."

"*My* claim?" Heath sounded taken aback. "You're part of this family. This involves you just as much as it does me."

"Sure." A lump formed in Nolan's throat. His relationship with Heath was neither straightforward nor easy, but that didn't stop Nolan from wanting to improve it. "But I've been gone so long I didn't really think you considered me part of the family anymore."

A silence greeted his statement while both men processed the doubts that Nolan had dared to voice.

"I'm sorry you feel that way," Heath said at last. "I'll admit that it's been hard without you around all these years, but Mom often reminded me that you had your own path to follow. You always did have a restless nature, and there's not a lot of new ground to discover here in Royal."

An overwhelming surge of relief and sorrow washed over Nolan. For the first time since he'd returned home, Nolan felt as if Heath at least understood his need to leave Royal, even if he didn't like that his twin had gone.

"I'm sorry I took off and left you holding the bag."

Heath huffed. "I don't believe that for a second. You always had your eyes on the horizon. I can't imagine that you gave any thought to how I would take being left here without you."

Nolan winced at the shotgun blast of guilt his brother had unloaded on him. "Actually, I did think about it," he said, forcing down his resentment. "I almost didn't leave, but then I thought about how miserable I would be and how you had everything under control with the ranch. Also, I never expected to be gone so long. I thought I'd see some of the world and eventually come home. Turns out there was more world for me to see than I anticipated."

"Considering we're twins, you and I are completely different people," Heath said, sounding unusually thoughtful. "The ranch is where I belong. I have no interest in leaving Royal. Even with all the troubles we've had in the last few years, with the storms and droughts, and then losing Mom and Ashley, I never even thought about selling and doing something else."

"Of course not," Nolan agreed, unable to imagine Heath as anything but a rancher. "You were made to be a cattleman."

"So, Chelsea Grandin agreed to go on a date with you," Heath mused, bringing them back to the original topic. "Interesting."

"We hit it off."

"I wouldn't have guessed you'd have any luck with her."

"I'll be honest, I'm a little surprised myself." Despite their significant chemistry, Nolan presumed the trouble between their families would've been too great a barrier. "But she was definitely into me."

"She's a little too practical to be swept off her feet," Heath said, his voice dry. "Even by a charmer like you."

"So what are you saying?" Even as he asked, Nolan anticipated Heath's answer.

"That she might be using you the same way you're using her."

"That occurred to me." Nolan decided to play it cool. Heath had made it clear that he didn't trust any of the Grandin family. No need for Nolan to divulge his eagerness to get acquainted with Chelsea. "But she also might be looking to have a little fun."

"That doesn't sound like Chelsea," Heath said. "She's the most sensible of all her siblings. And she's devoted to the Grandin Ranch. She'll go to great lengths to keep it safe."

"Including dating me?" Nolan cursed the trace of disappointment audible in his voice. Although he recognized that his brother was right to be cautious, Nolan was convinced that the attraction between them was real.

Heath waited a beat before replying, "Just watch yourself."

"I'll be careful."

* * *

"Where are you off to?" Chelsea's mother looked up from the crossword puzzle she been working on. Her eyes widened as she took in her oldest daughter. "Dressed like that?"

For her first date with Nolan, Chelsea had decided on a body-hugging long-sleeved dress in midnight blue with a reverse V neckline. Viewed from the front, she looked sexy but covered up from collarbone to knee. The drama came when she turned away—a gold zipper ran from the low point of the back V to the hemline, just begging to be undone. She'd gotten a little thrill putting it on and imagining Nolan's reaction. Would he see it as an invitation or a challenge?

"I'm having dinner with somebody." Chelsea was proud of her nonchalant tone, even though her insides were churning with excitement and anxiety.

"She's having dinner with Nolan Thurston," Layla piped up. She'd come for dinner since her fiancé was working late.

"You're dating a Thurston? Why would you do that with everything that's going on?" Her mother looked scandalized.

Chelsea shot her sister a withering glance. She'd explained to Layla her plan to go out with Nolan in order to gather some inside information on his brother's strategy regarding the oil rights. Since Layla had been Nolan's first target a couple months earlier, Chelsea had been hoping to get some insight from her sister.

"You could have your pick of any bachelor in

town," her mother continued. "Why did you choose someone who is trying to ruin us?"

"It's for that exact reason that I'm going out with him." Chelsea hated feeling like a misguided teenager. Why couldn't her family ever see her as an intelligent, competent individual who knew exactly what she was doing? "Honestly, you can't seriously believe I'd be interested in dating him otherwise."

"Well." Bethany sniffed. "You don't have the best track record when it comes to picking men."

Chelsea didn't need to be reminded of her woeful dating blunders. She'd had more than her fair share of being ghosted by men she'd dated. It had happened often enough to make her reluctant to go out with anyone. But Nolan was different. She wasn't actually dating him.

"I'm hoping to get some insight into what he and Heath are planning."

Layla smirked. "If he's anything like his brother, he's not gonna tell you a thing."

"You don't know that," Chelsea fumed. "We had—" Damn. It sounded idiotic to say it, but what the hell. "—a connection."

"It's more likely that he's going to try and use you to get information the same way he tried when he asked Layla for a lunch date," her mother said, sending a speaking glance her daughter's way.

"Hey!" Layla exclaimed. "I knew exactly what he was up to, and I'm sure Chelsea does as well."

"I do," Chelsea agreed. "I don't need any of you worrying about me. Sometimes I think you all forget that I'm a capable thirty-five-year-old woman who knows how to take care of herself and this ranch."

"You should just let your father and Vic take care of this oil rights business," her mother said, returning to her puzzle.

Chelsea ground her teeth together, frustrated by her mother's persistent exclusion of Chelsea's participation in major decisions surrounding the ranch. It was bad enough that her father and grandfather had clung to the notion that a male heir should be in charge, but Bethany Grandin was just as old-fashioned.

Just because their mother's sole ambition in life was to marry a rich rancher and manage his personal life didn't mean that her daughters were cut from the same cloth. Not that she'd stood in the way of Morgan opening the Rancher's Daughter. It was just when it came to Chelsea's dream of running the ranch that her mother couldn't get on board.

It stung that none of her family valued her input or gave her any credit. Especially after the changes she'd made to the land and animal management had improved the quality of the stock they raised. How maddening that her father refused to acknowledge a more efficiently and productively run ranch if it meant that any of the daughters—and not the son—were responsible for the improvements. To Chelsea's mind, this was incredibly shortsighted. But what could she do when her parents' mindsets were firmly entrenched in traditional patriarchy?

"Besides," Chelsea continued, tabling her resentment for another time. "Haven't you heard the old saying 'keep your friends close and your enemies closer'?"

"Which category does Nolan fall into?" Layla asked, arching a skeptical brow.

"Do I really need to answer that?" Chelsea snapped, rising to her sister's bait.

"Just watch yourself," her mother said. "Those Thurston boys are out for blood."

Chelsea thought over her initial meeting with Nolan. While her mother had every reason to judge the brothers harshly, Chelsea couldn't help but wonder if they had the Thurston twins pegged accurately. Sure, their potential ownership of the oil rights threatened the ranch, and that of their neighbors and dear friends the Lattimores. But wasn't it possible that Nolan and Heath were couching the matter as a business venture rather than some sort of vendetta.

On the heels of that question came the realization that she was already giving Nolan the benefit of the doubt—and that was certain to play straight into his hands.

No, her family was right. Chelsea needed to keep her wits about her. She had too much to prove and their ranch to save.

"I didn't fall for Nolan Thurston's charm," Layla said, coming to her sister's aid at last. "And neither will Chelsea."

Although Chelsea could see their mother wasn't convinced by anything she had heard in her daughter's defense, she left the ranch filled with a greater sense of determination. All her life she'd been living with her family's lack of faith in her. She hadn't let it get her down before. It certainly wasn't going to affect her now.

Chelsea had agreed to meet Nolan at the bench in front of the bank where they'd eaten their ice cream. She arrived five minutes early and discovered Nolan was waiting for her. She'd parked a block down and made her way slowly along Main Street. It had been months since she'd put on a pair of heels, and she was unaccustomed to walking in the five-inch stilettos.

"Wow!" He studied her with open admiration as she drew near. "I didn't think you could get any more beautiful, but I was wrong. You look gorgeous."

She'd styled her hair in artful, beachy waves and swept the entire curtain over her left shoulder. With her large eyes, strong bone structure and overly wide mouth, Chelsea knew she was more striking than beautiful.

For a long time she'd resented her ugly duckling status and the praise her prettier sisters received. While she'd eventually made peace with her shortcomings and learned to enhance her best features, being told she was beautiful by a handsome guy who also happened to be sexy and charismatic was going straight to her head.

"You look pretty great yourself." She took in his charcoal-gray suit and black button-down shirt. The dark shades combined with his swarthy complexion gave him an edgy look. With the top button of his shirt undone, it was a struggle to tear her gaze away from the exposed hollow of his throat. If his dimples hadn't been flashing, she would've reconsidered going anywhere alone with him. "I was a little worried that I might've overdressed."

Taking her hand in a familiar grip, he leaned forward and placed a warm kiss on her cheek. A searing zing snatched her breath away. Feeling as giddy and idiotic as a naive teenager on her first date, Chelsea wondered what had come over her. Was she really this susceptible to the man's over-the-top sex appeal?

"You're perfect." Another sizzling smile melted her bones as he gestured toward a rugged black Jeep that looked like it could tackle any terrain Texas decided to throw at it. "Shall we go?"

"Sure." Chelsea had nearly reached the passenger door before realizing that Nolan hadn't followed her. Wondering if she'd mistaken which car he'd meant, she turned and found him rooted to the sidewalk, his espresso eyes wide, his full lips pursed in a silent whistle. "Are you okay?"

"Am I okay?" He set his palm against his chest and staggered dramatically. "That dress is the sexiest thing I've seen all year. When you walked away, you nearly killed me."

"Did I?"

As Nolan strode her way, Chelsea caught herself grinning with feminine satisfaction. Okay, she'd achieved the exact effect she'd been after, but was it merely delight that her plan was working or was she testing her sexual power on a man she desired?

She might be in trouble if she was doing something

other than scoping out how much Nolan knew about his brother's intentions or discovering the truth of his mother's connection to her uncle Daniel. Better still if she could convince him to leave her family's ranch alone—or persuade him to encourage Heath to drop the claim. Her main purpose in dating him was to achieve any or all of these goals and to prove to her family once and for all that Grandin Ranch should be hers.

But as Nolan reached her side and skimmed his fingertips along her spine, to the top of the zipper, and gave the tab a little tug, she wasn't sure where ambition stopped and hunger began. Trembling with yearning, she bit her lip. The temptation to beg him to unfasten the zipper was both dangerous and all-consuming.

Nolan lowered his head and murmured, "Sexy as hell, Ms. Dreamy."

The endearment tickled her. "Isn't it a little early for nicknames?" she queried in a shaky rush as his breath puffed against her neck.

"I call 'em as I see 'em. And you are definitely as dreamy as they come."

Four

Damn the woman, Nolan thought with grudging admiration as he fingered the tab at the top of the zipper. He hadn't been exaggerating when he declared that she'd nearly killed him with this dress. As soon as he saw that gold zipper stretching from neckline to hem, all he could think about was snatching the tab and sliding it all the way down. She'd caught him off guard, and that rarely happened these days.

Maybe she needed a lesson in what happened when he was provoked.

He slid his finger along the vein in her neck, feeling as well as hearing her breath catch. Her eyes lifted to meet his, and her look was direct and unwavering. Not quite a challenge, but not exactly consent. But then she leaned just ever so slightly in his direction, and he saw an invitation in the subtle curve of her lips.

Now it was his breath's turn to hitch. Rationally, he knew they were playing a game, but she'd reeled him in. Before he could give in and taste her, Heath's warning blasted through his mind.

She might be using you the way you're using her.

Nolan pulled back before temptation led him into trouble. "You know, we never properly introduced ourselves."

She nodded, as if seeing where he was going. "Chelsea Grandin."

"Nolan Thurston." He watched her reaction to his name and saw no surprise. So, she had known who he was from the start. "Is this going to be a problem?"

"Probably." Her wry smile made his pulse race. "I'll just have to see if you're worth it."

Her reply stunned him into laughter. "I guess I'll have to be on my best behavior."

With that out of the way, he helped her into the passenger seat and circled to the driver's side. Nolan appreciated the brief respite to restore his equilibrium. Chelsea Grandin had taken a blowtorch to his cool control, and he had to figure out the best way to find his way back.

"Where are we off to?" she asked as he backed out of the parking space and headed for the highway leading out of town.

"I thought we'd have dinner at Cocott in downtown Dallas. I've heard the food is pretty good."

"Cocott?" Chelsea's frown was equal parts con-

fused and concerned. "You do realize that it's so popular it's impossible to get a reservation."

Nolan nodded. "I've heard that."

"So...do you have a reservation?"

"I do." Nolan shot her a smug grin. "I'll bet you're
dying to know my secret."

"I am curious."

"The owner is a friend of mine. I don't know if
you're familiar with the travel show *Fork and Backpack*? I worked on it with Camila Darvas. She and
I crisscrossed France for several months while she
filmed it." The series had featured the cuisine and
culture of small towns, and he'd had a blast learning
about the various regions in France. "She opened Cocott shortly after the show aired, and it sounds like
the restaurant is doing very well."

"What is it you do, exactly?"

"I scout international locations for television
shows. Reality TV mostly, but I've worked on a few
film projects as well."

"That's a very unusual career. And one that must
require a lot of travel."

"The amount changes every year and depends on
how busy I want to be. On average I'm on the road
thirty to forty weeks."

Chelsea's eyes went round. "I can't imagine being
away from home that long." Her gaze turned thoughtful. "Although I did go through a phase in high school
when I wanted to spend a year studying in Paris."

From her wistful expression, he could see she regretted not doing so.

"What happened?"

"I decided it didn't make sense if I intended on majoring in agriculture. Ranching is in my blood, and it's all I've ever wanted to do." She gave a half-hearted shrug. "How did you get started scouting locations for TV?"

"I was eighteen when I left Royal. I was a man without a plan. Maybe that helped me. I don't know. I was open to whatever opportunities came my way. All I knew is that I wanted to see more of the world."

Chelsea shuddered. "I don't know whether that's brave or insane, but I could never have taken a leap of faith like that."

"Don't forget I was just out of high school. And prone to rash behavior." Nolan thought back to those first few months living on his own and couldn't imagine too many people who'd embrace that sort of freedom. "I went to LA and took a job working on a private yacht as a deckhand. The captain took a liking to me, and when he got a boat in the Caribbean, he took me along. From there I got enough experience to bounce over to Europe, where I worked the summer in the Mediterranean. It was during a private charter off the Amalfi Coast that I met a studio head." Nolan smiled, remembering that fortuitous meeting. "Skip McGrath took a chance on me, and I never looked back."

"It must've taken a lot of courage for you to strike out on your own at such a young age. It was hard enough for me going off to college." She fiddled with her gold bracelet. "I have no idea how I would've survived the way you did."

"Everyone has their own path. Even though I got into several schools, college wasn't for me. My mom encouraged me to take a gap year to decide what I wanted to do with the rest of my life."

"I'll bet she never expected that you would go and never come back."

"Things might have ended up different if I hadn't stumbled into an industry that pays me very well to do what I love. Can't get much better than that."

"With that amount of traveling, how often do you get back to Royal?"

"I don't get back to Royal at all. My mother and sister's funeral two years ago was the first time I'd been back."

She gawked at him. "But why? Were you that busy or was it something else?"

Her question hit too close to home. He knew Chelsea was tight with her family. Hell, there were three generations of Grandins living together on that ranch. She probably could never imagine anything that would put them at odds.

"I felt like I let them down, given the way I left. And I wasn't sure I'd be welcome." Nolan wasn't sure what possessed him to confide such a painful truth, especially when he didn't know if he should trust her.

"What happened?"

"None of them knew about my plans to leave Royal until after I was gone." He nodded at her aghast expression. "It wasn't the best way to handle things, but I knew that it would be hard enough to go without them putting pressure on me to stay. And then the longer I stayed away, the harder it was for me to face coming home."

From Chelsea's stricken look, it was pretty clear that she perceived his absence as upsetting. No doubt someone who'd surrounded herself with family and never considered leaving Royal would find it hard to distance herself from home.

"Weren't you lonely?" She frowned. "I mean, what did you do for holidays?"

"I had friends who I spent time with. Also, a lot of times I was out of the country. I kinda got accustomed to it after a while. And I was always comfortable being alone."

"So you and Heath aren't close?"

Inwardly, Nolan flinched at her dismay. Her need for family and his need for individualism were at odds. It was just one of the many things they didn't have in common.

"I think people expect twins to be the same. Given the shared DNA and all. But Heath and I are quite different. I was held back a year before entering first grade."

"How come?"

"Heath and I were born on August 20, and my parents thought while Heath was ready for first grade, I wasn't." Although studies claimed that keeping a child back a year wouldn't affect him in the long run, the decision had caused a rift between the twins.

"That must've been an adjustment for you both."

"More so for me than Heath. We had different friend groups and were never studying the same subjects. I always felt as if I was behind him, even though we made similar grades all through school. It definitely meant we weren't as close as we had been."

"I guess that's why I didn't recall you growing up. I kinda remember Heath…"

No wonder. His brother had always been the more outgoing twin.

"I would've been a lowly freshman when you were a senior. Even if we'd gone to the same high school, I wouldn't have expected you to give me the time of day."

"I'm sorry." She sounded more confused than apologetic. "I feel like I should've noticed you. I mean, Royal isn't that big."

He was unsure if she was merely flirting with him or if he should trust the confusion underlying her remark. She genuinely seemed perplexed by her limited memory of him.

Nolan's own recollection was quite different. Chelsea had been a cheerleader and president of her school's student council, and pretty in a way that had started his teenage hormones buzzing. "A two-year age gap isn't anything now," he said, "but back then it was a lifetime. I'm not surprised at all that you don't remember me."

"I guess you're right. Huh."

Her pensive expression faded away, replaced by a dawning realization. She fixed her keen brown gaze on him and quirked an eyebrow. But whatever was turning over in her mind remained unspoken.

"What are you thinking?" he prompted, intrigued by the vibes rolling off her.

Her brow puckered. "I've never dated a younger man before."

The level of sexual tension between them ratcheted up a notch as she bit her lip and shot him a smoky glance. Nolan was having a hard time keeping track of his purpose in asking her out tonight. Heath had described Chelsea Grandin in a way that didn't jibe with the flesh-and-blood woman seated beside him.

"Seems like you might be interested in giving it a try." At least, he sure as hell hoped that was the case.

Her low hum filled the car as she gave the matter serious thought. "I think I just might."

Cocott definitely lived up to its stellar reputation. The decor was simple—dark gray walls adorned with enormous sepia images of Paris. Indirect lighting in the tray ceiling. Basic white tablecloths. A votive candle glowing on each table. The star of Cocott was the exquisite food.

The hostess led the way to a table in the back and left them with a warm smile. Nolan gallantly helped Chelsea settle into her seat before taking the chair opposite her.

"No menus?" She looked at Nolan in confusion.

He shrugged. "When I called Camila, she said she'd prepare something special for us."

"Mysterious," Chelsea murmured, a little thrill chasing across her skin.

She'd suspected that tonight's dinner would be one to remember, but she hadn't anticipated this level of intrigue. Then again, she'd never imagined Nolan would be well-connected enough to get a reservation at a place like Cocott, much less secure them a private tasting by a world-renowned chef. If the man was trying to impress her, he'd scored huge.

As she was mulling over her dinner companion, a waiter arrived with a bottle of wine.

"Good evening. I understand you are special guests of Cocott tonight." The man had salt-and-pepper hair and a lean smile. "My name is Richard, and I will be your waiter. Chef Darvas has prepared a special menu for you tonight. Starting off, I have a pinot gris from Alsace for you."

What followed was course after course of the most delicious food Chelsea had ever eaten. Seared Hudson Valley foie gras, a salad with kale and white truffle honey, and then salmon with leeks, dandelion and green apple.

While they ate, Nolan described his months of travel with Camila and all the fascinating places she'd taken him. The stories stirred young Chelsea's longing for a year spent studying abroad, and she wondered how her life would be different if she'd let her heart guide her instead of her head.

As the waiter was taking away their empty entrée plates, a beautiful woman in chef's whites approached their table. Given the success of her television show and this Dallas restaurant, Chelsea had expected a much older woman. Instead, Camila Darvas looked to be close to Chelsea's age, thirty-five. Since Nolan had his back to the kitchen, he didn't see the chef approach until Camila set her hand on his shoulder. Nolan sprang to his feet and exchanged a set of cheek kisses with her before throwing his arm wide to introduce Chelsea.

"Nice to meet you," Camila said in her accented English, her warm smile encompassing both Nolan and Chelsea.

"Your food was fantastic," Chelsea gushed, liking the Frenchwoman immediately. "I'll be honest, my sisters and I have been dying to come here, but getting a reservation is nearly impossible."

"I'm so glad you enjoyed it," Camila said. "I was a little surprised when Nolan called me to say he had someone he wanted to bring to my restaurant."

"Why is that?"

"When we traveled together, he didn't exactly appreciate my cooking."

"How is that possible?" Chelsea gaped at Nolan. "Her food is fantastic."

"I'm not a fan of all the sauces."

An affectionate look passed between Camila and Nolan that made Chelsea's heart clench. Had they been lovers? If the talented chef was Nolan's type, Chelsea questioned why he'd be interested in her. Wouldn't he be drawn to someone who shared his passion for travel and adventure? Did this confirm that he really wasn't attracted to her at all, but that he was only using her because of the oil rights?

Chelsea's chaotic thoughts were interrupted by the arrival of dessert. Her mouth watered as Camila described the final course, a bittersweet chocolate marquise with anise-scented cherries and crème fraîche ice cream.

"Nolan said you enjoyed chocolate," Camila said, her hand on the back of his chair. "I think you'll really enjoy this dessert."

"I'm sure I will," Chelsea assured the chef even as she told herself to not get too excited that Nolan had noticed her love of all things chocolate.

With a fond smile for Nolan, Camila took herself back to her kitchen. As much as Chelsea had liked the chef, she was glad the woman was gone. While meeting her had been enjoyable, it had also raised too many questions when it came to Nolan.

If he noticed that she was quieter on the way back to Royal, Nolan made no mention of it. Perhaps he assumed she was in a food coma, which wasn't far from the case. The delicious meal, combined with the different wine pairings with each course, had put Chelsea in a blissful physical state that lasted until they arrived in Royal.

"I'm parked over there." She indicated her truck, dreading the evening's end.

Despite the disquiet fluttering over Nolan's motivation for asking her out, she'd had a wonderful time. Far better than she'd expected. The type of man she usually dated had a stable profession, was pragmatic and tended to be a little dull. Nolan had fascinated her with stories of the exotic locations he'd visited, and his disarming charm had put her at ease. His adventurous spirit had sparked something restless inside her, and that, combined with her earlier worries about his reasons for asking her out, made her more than a little uncomfortable.

So, what was her next move?

Tonight, as if by mutual assent, they'd steered clear of all talk of the oil rights he and his brother were pursuing. If her whole purpose in dating him was to find out what they planned to do next, she'd abjectly failed. Instead, she'd flirted away as if she'd been on a regular date. She couldn't trust him. Planned on using him. And must avoid getting burned in the process. But damn if she didn't want a good-night kiss.

While she'd been locked in a fierce battle between her head and her hormones, Nolan had brought the Jeep to a stop behind her pickup and thrown the vehicle into Park. He turned his torso to face her. As they stared at each other in silence, Chelsea wondered if he, too, was struggling with how to end the date.

Nolan broke the silence. "Thank you for tonight."

His deep voice rumbled through her like an earthquake. She quivered in the aftermath.

"That's supposed to be my line," she responded, devouring his strong masculine features with her gaze, appreciating how his well-shaped lips softened into a small smile. Chelsea was pretty sure she could drown in his dreamy brown eyes. Had she ever dedicated so much energy to just appreciating the way a man looked? "Thank you for dinner. It was just perfect."

"I'm glad you enjoyed it."

"I really did."

Impulsively, she cupped his cheek in her palm. He drew in a sharp breath but didn't move a muscle. Her stomach clenched at the intense light in his gaze.

"I'd really like it if you would kiss me," she said, unsure when she'd decided to go off script.

"I can do that."

She stroked her thumb over his lower lip, tugging at it. "A slow kiss. One that tells me I am worth breaking the rules for."

She didn't explain what rules, but he had to recognize what they were doing was going to make their respective families unhappy. She was convinced this was why he'd decide to take her to Dallas for dinner rather than dine at one of Royal's excellent restaurants. The fewer people that saw them together, the easier it would be to deny they were dating.

If that's indeed what they were doing. Dating. Her breath hitched. Worry intruded. Maybe his mind was on something different. One way to find out…

She tilted her face and leaned ever so slightly toward him. To her relief, he dipped his head and stroked his lips against hers in the softest, most tender of kisses. The gentleness made her senses ignite. She wanted more. For his lips to own her. His hands to learn every inch of her skin. For his tongue to glide over all her sensitive areas.

Moaning as hunger flared between her thighs,

Chelsea sank her fingers into the soft texture of his hair and pressed hard into his mouth. He groaned low and deep, and suddenly he was with her in the kiss, sliding his tongue across her lower lip, taking the tender flesh between his teeth and then claiming her with a deeper contact that she could feel sizzling through every cell in her body. Feverish and wild, she longed for more, for him to slam her against a wall and run his hands all over her.

By the time he broke off the kiss, Chelsea had lost track of time and place. Groggily, she opened her eyes and caught sight of her surroundings. Whoa. She and Nolan had been making out like horny teenagers in full view of anyone wandering Main Street at nine o'clock at night.

She cursed.

"You okay?" he asked, holding her face with the tips of his fingers.

It took a huge amount of willpower to pull away. "Perfectly fine. It's just this is pretty public…"

"And Royal is a small town." He nodded in understanding. "It's still early. Do you want to go back to my place?"

Chelsea immediately perked up at his offer. She'd enjoyed spending time with Nolan and really didn't want to head home so early. "I'd like that."

Whoops. Did agreeing to go back to his place after that passionate kiss give him the idea that she intended to sleep with him on the first date? She'd better correct that assumption fast. Still, she hesitated. All too often she was criticized for speaking her mind. Would being blunt turn him off? Or maybe she didn't need to worry with Nolan. He seemed the sort of guy who could handle a little straightforward communication.

"Uh-oh," Nolan said, peering at her with a slight pucker between his eyebrows. "What's wrong?"

Chelsea blinked. "Wrong?"

"You got really serious all of a sudden."

"Oh."

She focused on his handsome face, and the concern reflected in his gaze made her want to start kissing him all over again. Damn the man for seeming too good to be true.

"I don't want you to get the wrong idea." Despite her best intentions, heat rose up her throat and burned in her face. Still, she managed to keep her tone casual. "I'm not agreeing to sleep with you."

To her relief, his teeth flashed in a broad smile. "Ever?" he teased.

The warmth in her cheeks lanced straight to her belly and coiled there like a purring cat. The vibration hit all the right spots, turning her on like crazy.

"Not tonight."

When his dimples flashed, she realized what she'd given away. Her mouth popped open, but it was too late to take it back. A second later she decided she didn't want to. Her body longed for Nolan Thurston. Good or bad, she was not strong enough to withstand the attraction between them. She just hoped when she gave in, she'd be able to survive the coming storm.

Five

"I'm surprised you're not staying at your family's ranch," Chelsea said, glancing around the loft's open floor plan. Her gaze ricocheted off the king-size bed at the far end before returning her attention to him.

They sat sideways on his couch, facing each other, their knees a whisper apart. The energy between them crackled and popped. Nolan drank in the bold drama of her features and traced the length of her slender neck to the delicate hollow of her throat. He recalled the graceful flare of her shoulder blades and the gentle wave of her spinal column as it disappeared behind that tantalizing gold zipper.

"I thought it might be a lot to expect that I would stay there after being gone for fifteen years."

Nolan hoped he'd imagined the fleeting speculation in her eyes at his remark. He wanted to believe that she was here without an agenda.

"So, how come you're still single?" he asked, deciding to distract her with personal questions. "Is every man in Royal blind?"

A startled laugh burst from her. "Thanks for the compliment, but once you get to know me better, I'm sure you'll realize that I'm no one's idea of a catch."

"Not from where I'm sitting." Nolan cocked his head and tried to suss her out. "If you're single, it's because that's the way you want it."

"Let's just say I'm so focused on the ranch that my personal life suffers." She smoothed her palm along her skirt.

He leaned his upper body forward and spoke softly. "Maybe you just haven't found the right guy."

The way her lashes fluttered and gaze zipped away, Nolan sensed he'd struck at a sore spot. Given her strong will and confident nature, he couldn't imagine any guy getting away with breaking her heart or bruising her spirit. Could he be wrong?

"Sure..." After grappling with something, she released a huge sigh. "Or I'm the problem."

Her admission startled him. Obviously, she had a story to tell. Still to be determined was whether she wanted to share it with him.

"Why would you say that?"

"The men I date have a tendency to disappear."

"Maybe you have a secret admirer who's taking them out." He made an exaggerated martial arts move with his hands and drew a faint smile from her.

"It's more like they dump me for someone less complicated and demanding to date."

"Or they're not man enough to handle an intelligent, accomplished woman."

"And it's really not that things don't work out," Chelsea said, her lips tightening with remembered annoyance. "It's more that instead of having a conversation and breaking up like civilized people, they ghost me. A couple of enjoyable dates where it feels like something might be developing, and then nothing."

"That's a crappy thing to do," Nolan said even as he wondered if he'd been guilty of that in his past. He'd assumed the women he'd gone out with had understood the nature of his business, but it was possible he'd vanished from their lives in a similarly abrupt way. "How many times has it happened?"

"Four. But the worst was Brandon. We'd dated several months before he disappeared. And I think I'm making it worse because I expect it now. I have a really hard time trusting anyone, and that gives men the impression that I'm an iceberg."

"But you're not." Half statement, half assurance. Nolan felt her relax and knew he'd struck the right note. "Trust me. That kiss earlier was dynamite, and the chemistry I feel with you tells me that you're a smoldering volcano."

"You are great for my ego," she told him with a wry smile that didn't quite mask her relief. "And a breath of fresh air."

"Maybe what you need is to date someone different from your usual type. What sort of guys do you usually go for?"

"I gravitate toward serious types who are focused on business. Men like my dad, I guess." She looked slightly dazed by her sudden insight. "As much as it drives me crazy that he's so traditional, I keep dating men that don't appreciate women who are serious about their careers."

"And that's not you."

"Far from it. I'm always trying to do things better. Most of the time I forget that every second of my day and every thought in my head doesn't have to revolve around cattle."

Nolan reached out and took her hand in his. Turning it palm up, he drew circles on her skin. "Sounds like you haven't met anybody who could take your mind off your problems."

"It's not an easy thing to do." Her lashes fluttered at his caress, and rosy color stole into her cheeks. "I'm always working twice as hard as my brother to get noticed." She made a face and looked uncomfortable with the admission.

"Why are you competing with your brother?" Nolan smiled as his light touch lured her into revealing more about her family dynamic. "It seems to make sense that as the oldest you'd be in charge."

"It's my dad. I described him as traditional." She bit her lower lip as he slid his fingers between hers. The contact was disrupting her wariness and loosening her tongue. "He believes the only person who deserves to be in charge of the ranch is a man. That means my brother."

"That seems very shortsighted of him. There are four of you, right?"

Chelsea studied their entwined hands. "Three girls and one boy. My youngest sister, Morgan, has no interest in running the ranch. She owns a boutique on Main Street. The Rancher's Daughter." With her free hand, Chelsea indicated what she was wearing. "This dress is from there."

"I think you already know my opinion of it," Nolan murmured.

"I don't dress up very often anymore." Chelsea made a face. "After Brandon ghosted me two years ago, my parents started pushing eligible men at me. I think they hoped I'd find a husband." The disgust in her voice came through loud and clear. Clearly this was not her goal.

"You don't want to get married?"

"I don't have anything against it." Chelsea shrugged. "But I don't like my parents' assumption that it's what I was born to do."

Obviously, she was a modern woman whose contemporary ideas were in conflict with her family's perception of what their daughter ought to do.

Chelsea grimaced. "Maybe that's why I've put my personal life on hold. The last thing I want to do is prove my parents right. At least not until I've achieved my goal of taking charge of the ranch. Even though it's an uphill battle, I'm convinced that I'd be completely out of the running if I started dating someone my family found acceptable."

Although Nolan doubted she meant to point out that her family would never approve of him, she had to be thinking about it. As the brother of the man who was trying to interfere with the smooth running of her ranch, she was courting trouble by not keeping her distance.

Of course, this left him wondering if, for all her casual air, she had an ulterior motive for being here with him. His chest constricted as disappointment trickled through him. He had no reason to feel this way. Hadn't he approached her with the idea of getting into her good graces and finding her family's weaknesses?

"I'm not sure why I told you that," she murmured, tunneling her fingers into her hair and giving the dark locks a sharp tug.

"You're not what I expected," he said spontaneously.

"No?" She tensed. A frown appeared to mar her smooth forehead.

He immediately saw that his offhand remark had made her wary and recalled what she'd revealed of her insecurity. "You have a reputation around town for being all business. I thought I'd have a hard time getting to know you."

She let loose a rusty laugh. "I guess that's a fair assessment. My focus has always been my family's ranch. I went to college to study ranch and animal management with the intention that I would be in charge someday." A dark cloud passed across her features.

He thought of his own ambitions and how Heath had stepped up when their dad died. "It was never a question between Heath and me. He was always going to run our ranch."

"So he's older?"

"By about fifteen minutes."

"You two never considered sharing responsibility?"

Nolan shook his head. "Never. I wasn't keen on ranching, and Heath likes to do things his own way." He paused and shot her a wry smile. She was a lot like his brother. Another thing that might cause trouble between them in the future. "It worked out for both of us," Nolan continued. "Heath got the ranch, and I was free to let my wanderlust run wild."

Chelsea sighed. "I wish my brother, Vic, felt the way you do."

"You mean you wish he would give you the ranch and go do something else?"

"Frankly, yes. I'm the one with the passion for ranching." She practically growled the last word.

Obviously, Nolan could tell this was a sore subject, but one that provided much-needed insight into the Grandin family dynamic. "Does he want to be in charge?"

"I'm not sure he wants it the way I do. He's just always assumed the ranch would come to him. It's frustrating. Between all my siblings, I have the best vision for where the ranch should go. Yet my father can't imagine handing over the reins to me. I don't know if he assumes I'll one day get married and move out." Resentment poured off her in waves, an abrupt shift from the mellow mood she'd been in all evening. "It's what Layla has done. She and Joshua are getting a ranch of their own. What my dad doesn't understand is that he left her no other choice."

As if concluding that she'd shared enough about her family, Chelsea turned the conversation to things Nolan enjoyed doing when not traveling. She seemed unsurprised that his favorite activities involved adventure and often took him off the beaten path. Several times he glimpsed a wistful flicker in her eyes as he shared his pastimes. It was almost as if she regretted the lack of excitement in her life. This didn't seem to jibe with the no-nonsense businesswoman Heath had described. Nolan was quickly discovering that Chelsea Grandin was beautiful, intelligent and complicated.

"I should probably get going," Chelsea said, indicating the large, decorative wall clock. She slipped her feet from beneath her and settled them into her high heels. "I can't believe it's two in the morning."

Although he was loath to end the evening, he stood and held his hand out to assist her. "It's pretty late. Why don't I walk you down to your car?"

Up until the offer spilled from his lips, he'd planned to escort her as far as his front door and say goodbye with a lingering kiss that would leave her craving another date with him. But as he opened the condo door and gestured her through, Nolan could already feel himself missing her. The ache unsettled him.

Chelsea glanced up at him as she passed. "I'm sure I'll be okay."

"I insist."

"That's very gentlemanly of you."

There was laughter in her voice and speculation in her gaze. Nolan hadn't figured out yet if Chelsea was wary because of her dating failures in the past or of him in particular. Maybe both.

"You'd be the first woman who'd think so."

"I don't believe that. I saw the way Camila looked at you tonight. She was very happy to see you."

"We never hooked up," Nolan confessed, sensing it was important to reassure Chelsea of this. As they strolled side by side along Main Street in the direction of her car, Nolan peered at her expression. "She's great fun to travel with, but I don't cross professional lines."

"What about after the show was done? Did you have any interest in seeing her?"

Nolan shook his head. "We are great friends, but that's it for me."

"Are you sure?" Chelsea stared at him as if she didn't believe he could be so clueless. "She's beautiful and talented. Or is it because she's here in Texas and you're based out of LA?"

"She's too serious for something casual, and I wasn't interested enough to want more."

"Huh." Chelsea looked as if his answer had thrown her.

"What?"

"Just huh."

His travels had given him plenty of opportunity to meet and romance women of all kinds. Not that he was a player. Far from it. He truly enjoyed the company of women and didn't put scoring as his top priority for spending time with any of them. It just seemed as if he drew women who enjoyed sex without strings. Uncomplicated fun. Which had been great in his twenties, but since turning thirty, he'd begun to feel a different sort of restlessness.

Sitting still for the last few months had given Nolan time to mull his future. He'd caught up with some of his high school friends—many married and starting families—and gained a different perspective on his love life. He'd never imagined himself going down that road. Settling down had never been his plan, but he couldn't deny that his old classmates really seemed to enjoy having someone to come home to.

Yet Nolan recognized that domestic bliss wasn't for him. He had a globe-trotting career that kept him on the go. Sustaining a relationship under those circumstances would take a special woman. One Nolan had yet to meet.

All of a sudden, Chelsea stopped walking, jolting Nolan out of his thoughts. Looking around, he realized they'd arrived at her car. She was seconds away from escaping. He couldn't let her go without something to dream about. Catching her arm, he drew her toward him. He set his forefinger beneath her chin to tilt her head up and dropped a light kiss on her full lips. A sigh puffed out of her as he dusted a second kiss across her cheek.

"Do you want to go out again?" she murmured, sounding drowsy and content. She'd rested her palms on his waist right above his belt, and her touch seared straight through his fine cotton shirt.

He kissed her earlobe and felt her shiver. "I was going to ask you the same thing."

"Great minds…"

"Tomorrow?"

She gusted out a chuckle. "It's already tomorrow. How about Friday?"

"You're going to make me wait three whole days?"

"I'm sure you'll manage." And then she was pulling free and turning toward her car.

Nolan received another gut-kicking glimpse of that damned gold zipper running down the length of her dress before she unlocked her truck and climbed in. There was something so damned sexy about a well-dressed woman in a pickup, he thought with a grin. He might have been out of Texas nearly half his life, but some things remained the same.

"Text me when you get home," he called to her before the driver's door shut.

Chelsea leaned out to frown at him. "I'll be fine."

"You're already better than fine," he insisted, a trace of steel entering his tone. "Text me."

"It'll take me half an hour. You might be asleep by then."

"I won't be able to sleep unless I know you're home safe." Seeing that his request had spurred some sort of conflict inside her, Nolan stepped up to her car door. "I know you are capable of taking care of yourself, but I always insist my staff check in at night when we're on location. Humor me."

Her eyes softened. "I'll text."

With a satisfied nod, Nolan stepped back and watched until she'd driven off. Then he headed back to his loft to ponder what he was going to do with the dreamy Chelsea Grandin.

Despite the late hour, Chelsea was wide-awake as she drove back to Grandin Ranch. Her senses buzzed in the aftermath of Nolan's kiss, a dangerous intoxicant for a levelheaded woman like her. What if she grew addicted to the high and lost her way? Maybe she was more tired than she realized. A couple kisses weren't going to turn her head. She was dating Nolan as a way of finding out more about the Thurston brothers and their strategy for going after the oil beneath her family's land. Yet it bothered her that she found him so attractive.

She'd learned a lot from Nolan, more than she'd expected. The most important item had been that the relationship between the brothers wasn't as tight as her family believed. Chelsea felt a rush of optimism. Maybe there was an opportunity to win Nolan to her side.

But how?

The obvious answer lay in the chemistry percolating between them. Unfortunately, tonight had demonstrated that she was woefully out of practice at flirting. Look how she'd confessed that she refused to fall in love until her father accepted her as an independent woman capable of running the ranch. She'd also shared how much she hated the way her parents had tried for years to set her up with every eligible man in the county.

Overcome with remembered humiliation, Chelsea clenched the steering wheel. Why couldn't her father open his eyes and see her as his equal instead of a commodity he could use to cement relationships in the community?

To her dismay, lights still burned in the living room when she got home. Wondering if her mother had left the light on as a courtesy or if someone was actually waiting up for her, she parked her truck and braced herself as she entered the house.

Vic sat in their father's favorite chair, acting like he was already head of the family. Irritation bloomed at the sight, but it was his scowl and the fact that he was obviously waiting up for her that caused heat to steal into her cheeks. Honestly, she'd done nothing wrong, yet here she was blushing like a wayward teenager.

"What are you doing dating Nolan Thurston?"

"Not that it's any of your business," she declared coolly over her shoulder, keeping her voice low, "but I'm not dating him. I'm looking out for our family's best interest."

"How? By getting into bed with the enemy?"

Chelsea counted to ten even as she kept walking toward her bedroom. She didn't owe Vic an explanation. Still, she should've expected that with her family on edge about the Thurston brothers, they would've discussed what she was up to.

Despite all she'd learned from Nolan, Chelsea wished she'd come straight home after dinner. Or anytime in the five hours that followed. No doubt rolling in after two in the morning looked suspiciously like she'd slept with Nolan. Hell, she couldn't even deny that's what she'd wanted to do. Chelsea couldn't remember the last time a man intrigued her the way Nolan did. He wasn't like any of the men around town. All the things he'd seen on his travels had inspired her imagination and made her question the way she'd let her ambition monopolize her life.

"I didn't get into bed with anyone," Chelsea said, cursing as she paused to defend herself rather than head straight to her bedroom.

"What do you call spending all night with Nolan Thurston?"

It hadn't been all night. Vic was just trying to push her buttons. And as usual, it was working.

"Reconnaissance." She forced her lips into a smirk while her stomach roiled at the picture she was painting of herself. Coming off strong and ruthless was a defense mechanism. Their father ran Grandin Ranch like his father before him, with an iron hand. If she expected to be taken seriously, she must appear tough and determined. "I think he's the key to getting through to Heath about dropping the claim."

Vic was looking less sure of himself. "Or it's just an excuse because you're into him."

Chelsea rolled her eyes. "Give me some credit." The phrasing of the comment made her wince. She shouldn't be asking Vic to give her the benefit of the doubt. She didn't need to convince him of anything.

"Everybody thinks you should stay away from him."

"Then everybody is wrong." Chelsea was used to fighting for recognition in her family, but this path she was walking with Nolan left her feeling more alone than ever. "Anyway, what does it matter? It's not like I'm going to ever stop fighting their claim. The destruction that would happen to our ranch if they lease those oil rights to a drilling company would ruin our land forever. *I'm* not gonna let that happen."

"Maybe, but what if you fall for him? Maybe he's planning to seduce you in the hopes that he can change your mind."

For a split second, Chelsea considered arguing further. But why bother wasting her breath when the power belonged to her father? "You know that everything is going to be in the hands of the lawyers."

"Still, it looks bad, you hanging out with the enemy and all."

"Then I guess I'll just have to be more careful about being seen in public with him." She meant the remark to be sarcastic, but Vic took her seriously.

"It'd be better if you didn't see him at all, but if you can get some intel, then I guess it might be worth doing whatever."

Doing whatever? Chelsea felt a little bit ill. Had she gone too hard at the do-whatever-it-takes-to-win attitude?

"I don't think you and I should discuss the topic of my spending time with Nolan Thurston anymore."

"Why not?" Vic smirked. "Afraid to admit I'm right?"

Her brother was a little too cocky when it came to throwing his weight around. Maybe if he worked harder than she did on the ranch she might feel differently, but he was assuming their father would put him in charge, and that left him resting on his laurels.

Mired in his sense of entitlement, Vic didn't push himself, and his unwillingness or inability to take the initiative, think things through and make decisions drove her crazy. She'd respect him more if he behaved as her equal instead of just insisting he was.

"Because I don't answer to you," she replied. "Which means it's none of your business."

Her phone chimed. Reflexively, she glanced at the incoming text and caught her breath. It was from Nolan. Her heart fluttered as she read his message.

Home yet, Ms. Dreamy?

Cursing the nickname and her breathless state, Chelsea fired off a response.

Just arrived.

I had a great time tonight.

Me too.

Sweet dreams!

You too.

The text exchange made her forget all about the argument with Vic.

"Is that Thurston?"

She tore her attention away from the phone, her irritation returning in a rush. "It's late, and I have to be up in three hours. Unless you want to oversee the feeding this morning? Believe me, I'd be happy to sleep in for a change."

"I've got my own work," Vic grumbled.

"Of course you do. So, I'll see you around ten?" And then before her brother could reply, she stepped into her room and closed the door in his face.

With adrenaline surging in the aftermath of her fight with Vic, she wondered how long it would take for her to get to the sweet dreams Nolan had wished for her. She smiled again as she recalled the brief exchange.

Was it worth using someone to achieve her goals? Of course, there was always the possibility that Nolan was using her in turn. If they were both playing an elaborate game of cat and mouse, she might be the one in danger of getting hurt. Was she brave enough to continue?

Once upon a time, she'd let her heart lead her down a treacherous romantic path. Given the strong chemistry between her and Nolan, it would be easy for her emotions to lead her astray once again. Dating him would be a lot less complicated if she kept in the front of her mind the myriad reasons they could never work out. That way she wouldn't give her heart a chance to betray her.

And yet, did any of that matter if she succeeded in preventing the Thurstons from acting on the oil rights? Her father couldn't help but notice if she saved the ranch. Then he would have no choice but to put her in charge.

Wasn't a little heartache worth achieving everything she'd been working for all along?

Six

Nolan glanced at the woman occupying his passenger seat. Today, Chelsea wore a buttery-yellow sundress with thin straps that showed off her toned arms. She had a body built by hard work. All lean muscle beneath smooth, tan skin. He loved her athleticism and suspected she was one of the few women he knew who could match him for endurance.

"Where are we off to today?" she asked as Royal disappeared behind them.

While it wasn't unusual for him to plan fun adventures—ferreting out once-in-a-lifetime experiences was what he did for a living—he wanted every date with Chelsea to be memorable. Still, as he'd helped her into the car, a glimpse of her long, sleek thighs had set his pulse to dancing. Every instinct shouted for Nolan to bail on his plans for the evening and head straight to his place.

"I have a special surprise for us."

He'd found a company that specialized in gondola rides in Irving, Texas. It wasn't Venice, but he hoped the Italian meal, served while cruising the city's Mandalay Canal and Lake Carolyn, would appeal to her. Normally the cruise lasted two hours, but he'd paid extra to double their time. He had no intention of rushing anything with Chelsea.

"Sounds quite mysterious," she replied, delight shimmering in her wide brown eyes. "Do I get a hint?"

"Nope. I want you to be surprised."

Nolan reached across the space between them and captured her hand. Her fingers meshed easily with his, as if they'd done this a hundred times, and he brushed a kiss across her knuckles. A slight tremor went through her at his romantic gesture, and he felt a spasm of guilt. She'd been hurt several times by men she'd thought she could trust, and he was doing his damnedest to tear down her walls.

Dating Chelsea was like walking a tightrope without a net. With their families soon to be engaged in some pretty hostile conflict over the oil rights Heath intended to claim, she had to wonder if Nolan had ulterior motives for taking her out. Her intelligence was one of her strongest features. Yet the chemistry between them was real, and she seemed to be going with it. Something like that was incredibly hard to fake, but he had to consider that she might be playing him in turn. Nolan hoped the latter wasn't true.

Even as the thought popped into his mind, he knew he was in trouble. When Heath no longer needed him, Nolan planned to go back to his regular life. And with Chelsea completely bound to her ranch—and her family—it was unlikely that she would give up either one to follow him around the world. Which meant he'd better not get any more attached to Chelsea Grandin.

This realization should've made it easier for Nolan to temper his interest in her. Yet the sexual energy between them was hungry and strong. And he wasn't all that good at resisting adventures. When something called to him, he had no choice but to answer. And what he sensed about Chelsea's hidden depths called to him. He wanted to explore everything about her and, once seized by determination, no challenge was too much.

Nolan just had to keep his fascination with her on the down low. No need for Heath to know that his brother had strayed from their original mission. As long as Heath thought Nolan was simply using Chelsea to get intel on the Grandin family, the fledgling relationship between the two brothers would remain untested. At least where Chelsea was concerned.

Heath's obsession with the oil rights was a different matter.

It wasn't that Nolan didn't want to pursue the claim. He just didn't understand why their mother had owned the rights for years and never once mentioned them or tried to do anything about them. Surely, the millions a contract like that would be worth could've helped in the days when the Thurston ranch had gone through hard times.

In Nolan's opinion, too many questions remained about the situation. He wished he understood what drove his brother's obsession. He sensed more to it than the potential of adding to his wealth. Yet every time Nolan tried to raise this point with his brother, Heath refused to discuss the matter. Not wanting to upset their tenuous rapport, Nolan squashed his curiosity. Heath wasn't responsible for their falling-out. Nolan's absence from Royal had put distance between them. That made repairing the rift Nolan's responsibility, and he wasn't going to fix anything by arguing with his brother.

"Ever been here?" Nolan asked an hour later as they strolled hand in hand toward the dock where the gondolas waited.

Her voice was husky with awe as she murmured, "I had no idea this existed."

A man dressed as a traditional gondolier smiled as they approached. "Good evening," the man intoned in a passable Italian accent and extended a single red rose to Chelsea. She accepted the token with a bemused expression and turned to glance over her shoulder at Nolan.

"We're going in that?" She nodded toward the long, narrow boat. Since it was evening, he'd opted to go with the traditional open gondola rather than one of the covered varieties.

"Since a trip to Venice was a little much for a second date, I thought this would do."

He shot her a sideways glance, eager for her approval. His heart clenched when she gave his fingers a brief, fierce squeeze.

"I absolutely love it."

"I'm glad."

The gondolier handed Chelsea into the boat, and as she settled in a comfortable seat at the middle, Nolan stepped in. While the waitstaff placed plates loaded with their three-course meal on the intimate table before them, Nolan scrutinized her expression and decided he'd chosen well. For someone who didn't stray far from home, he sensed that Chelsea was actually enjoying getting outside her comfort zone.

"To your first gondola ride," Nolan murmured as the boat glided away from the dock. He touched his champagne flute to hers, enjoying her delight.

"I could get used to this," Chelsea said, humming in appreciation as she eyed the delicious plates of food. "Although I'm not sure how we're supposed to get through so much."

"I ordered a variety of dishes, unsure which you'd prefer."

"I'm not sure, either. I think I'd like to taste everything."

With the sun dipping toward the horizon, the July heat eased as they skimmed across the lake surface. A light breeze ruffled the hair framing Chelsea's face, and he used the excuse to slide a sable strand behind her ear. With a long sigh, her soft body relaxed into his side.

"Earlier, when I said I could get used to this," Chelsea said, gazing at him from beneath her lashes, "I wasn't just talking about the food or the boat ride. I meant you."

Should he take her declaration at face value? This was only the second time they'd gone out, and while he was feeling the strong vibe between them, she might be deliberately trying to give him a false sense of security by pushing the impression that she was more into him than she was.

Before he could decide how to respond, she added, "I'm just not sure that's a good idea."

Nolan registered a silent curse. Just when he had her figured out, she switched things up. Was she truly conflicted, or was this just a bit of gamesmanship?

"It's sensible of you to feel that way."

"That's the trouble. I struggle to feel sensible when I'm with you." She spun the stem of her champagne flute with her fingers. "We haven't talked about what's going on between our families."

"We don't have to get involved," Nolan stated, ignoring the fact that he had already agreed to help Heath by gleaning her family's strategy for opposing the claim. "You've already said you don't have control when it comes to the ranch and the decisions being made."

"That's true." She tensed as he probed this sore spot. "But the same can't be said for you."

"Heath is the one who wants to claim the oil rights."

"Are you trying to tell me you'd walk away from millions of dollars?"

He heard her skepticism and for a second wondered if their pleasant evening was over before it began.

"Yes." That wasn't a lie. If the decision was left up to Nolan, he would drop the matter. "I've made enough money with my scouting company to live comfortably for many lifetimes. But my brother is determined to fight to the bitter end."

Chelsea let out a long, exaggerated sigh and shook her head. "I wish I understood why my grandfather and Augustus Lattimore turned over the oil rights to your mother. It makes no sense."

"Maybe it was for child support. She was pregnant with your uncle's child."

"Was she?" Chelsea stared out across the water. "Other than the right timing, there's no real proof that your half sister was Daniel's daughter. And he claims he didn't know Cynthia was pregnant."

"Or maybe he knew and fled to France all those years ago to avoid the responsibility." It wouldn't surprise him. Nolan was no stranger to running away from obligation, implied or not. "How come he didn't stick around to help your father run the ranch?"

"I could ask the same of you," Chelsea countered.

"Even if I'd wanted to stick around, I don't know how much Heath would've let me help."

The instant the words escaped his mouth, Nolan regretted it.

"You know, I've been wondering why you never came back to Royal all these years." Her eyes gleamed with curiosity. "Something happened between you and Heath, didn't it?"

"Not really between us. I don't honestly think he had a clue…"

Nolan didn't talk about his family with anyone. When asked, he usually gave a pat answer about how his family owned a ranch in Texas and that ranching wasn't his thing. He should've known that Chelsea could inspire him to spill more than he usually shared.

"Heath was Dad's right hand and spent every spare second following him around the ranch, learning how to run it. When Dad died, even though we were only in elementary school, Heath stepped up and helped Mom a lot, eventually taking over running of most things by high school." Nolan thought about the ranch journal his father had kept and how he'd specified that it should go to Heath.

"I know firsthand what it's like to compete with a sibling. Even though my father loved Heath and me equally, there was no question that they were more in sync."

Chelsea leaned into his understanding, and her head settled against his shoulder, as if to take comfort from being close.

"At the time, our mom couldn't afford to hire a manager, and besides, Heath was convinced that everything would fall apart without him overseeing the operations." Nolan recalled how he'd sometimes felt like an outsider when he and Heath did things with their father. Dad and elder son had so much in common and so much to say to each other that a lot of the time Nolan just retreated into his own imagination. "I was jealous."

"Jealous? Why?"

"He was always closer to my dad. They had so much in common, and I always felt like a third wheel. It caused me to pull away from them. Even my mom and sister." This fact hadn't occurred to him at the time, but looking back on it, especially after losing his mom and Ashley, he acknowledged that his resentment had caused him to build walls.

"I get that," Chelsea said. "I've never been close with my dad, either. While he showers my brother with his time and attention, I had to learn about ranching from the foreman and at college." She toyed with the silverware as she continued, "But what really kills me is when Vic gets the credit for things that I've done. I still remember the shock I felt when I realized that being the oldest gave me no extra edge. I committed to doing whatever it took to prove myself. The problem is, no matter how hard I work, my father is blind to my achievements."

"I'm sorry your dad is like that. Even though I wasn't interested in ranching, when it came to fishing or running around on ATVs, the three of us had a blast. There just wasn't always time for fun. In the end, it all worked out. I got to see the world, and Heath gets to run the ranch he loves."

"I guess we are just destined to find our way based on what we want out of life. You are interested in seeing the world, and I'm interested in running it." Her lips curved into a wry grin. "Or at least my corner of it."

It bummed Nolan out a little that they were both

so different in this way. Eventually, he would have to leave Texas. He couldn't ignore his business forever. Many of the projects in the works would begin to ramp up, and he would start to scout locations. He thought about traveling with her, sharing many of the places that he'd loved. But she was so tied to her ranch. And with her locked in competition with her brother, he couldn't imagine convincing her to leave it, even for a few weeks. Was it crazy that this was only their second date and he was already uncomfortable at the thought of leaving her behind?

"Have you ever considered doing anything else?" Nolan posed the question as much to himself as to her and was unprepared for the stark anxiety that streaked across her face.

"Lately, I've been spending a lot of time wondering what I'm going to do if my father hands the reins over to my brother."

Her admission took him by surprise. Nolan reached out and took her hand. "That won't happen. He's going to come around."

But even as he reassured her, part of Nolan was hoping that one day Chelsea might lose the ranch and be forced to look for something new. He'd recognized that his stories had ignited her sense of adventure, and he wondered if a future existed where he could convince her to leave Texas and venture into the big, wide world. With him.

Chelsea stood on the back porch of the ranch house and stared across the side yard in the direction of the twenty acres her grandfather had gifted her on her twenty-first birthday. She'd planned to build a house there and demonstrate to her family that she was dug in. Although she enjoyed her close connection with her family, having three generations living in fifteen thousand square feet made for little personal space or privacy. Liking the idea of owning a home where she could be separate, yet remain close to her family, she'd hired an architect to draw up plans, interviewed contractors and had even gone so far as to pick out finishes. Yet she'd never pulled the trigger. In part because these last few years she'd focused so exclusively on the ranch that there was neither time nor energy for anything else. Plus, with her grandparents aging, she knew her time with them was limited.

Now, however, since starting to date Nolan, she wished she'd gone forward with the house. Every time she left for or came in from one of their dates, she ran into someone with an opinion about her activities.

"Chelsea!"

At the sound of her name, she wrenched herself out of her thoughts. Turning her head, she spied Layla standing beside her. "Sorry?"

The entire Grandin family had gathered for Sunday dinner to talk about the Thurston brothers and the oil rights claim. Anticipating the dread moment when the conversation would turn to her decision to date Nolan, she'd almost given in to his dinner invitation and bailed on her family. Instead, for the last hour, over predinner cocktails, she'd been defending her actions and reiterating her motivation while each one of her family members—with the exception of her grandmother Miriam, who at eighty-eight was having health issues—had dumped a truckload of censure upon her.

Simmering with frustration, she'd escaped to the back deck to cool off before dinner.

Her sister frowned. "I've been talking to you for ten minutes."

"Sorry."

"What is up with you? You've been so distracted lately." Layla gave her an odd look. "Ever since you met Nolan Thurston. It's like you're into the guy."

With her stomach in knots, Chelsea shrugged dismissively. "If I'm fooling you, then he's not going to catch on to what I'm doing."

"Are you sure it's him you're fooling?"

Chelsea sucked in a sharp breath. "What is that supposed to mean?"

"It's just that he's really different from all the guys you've dated before. It wouldn't surprise me if you fell for all his smoldering sexiness and masculine arrogance."

"I mean, he's sexy, sure." Her sister's description of Nolan made Chelsea frown. "But I don't see him as arrogant."

In fact, being with him left her awash in comfort. He seemed to understand her better than her family did. Having someone on her side was amazing. So much so that it only felt the littlest bit scary to let her guard down and allow herself be taken care of for a change.

Layla rolled her eyes. "Are you kidding? When he approached me a couple months ago, he was all, 'You and I should go out to lunch and discuss the oil rights claim. And bring your sister.'"

The commanding baritone Layla adopted sounded nothing like the Nolan Chelsea had been dating. Goose bumps rose on her arm. Was it possible that she wasn't seeing his true self? It wasn't unimaginable that he was playing her. In fact, the thought had crossed her mind often. After all, she was playing him.

As much as she wanted to reject her sister's insight, Chelsea would be unwise to ignore this reminder to be careful. If only it wasn't so easy to forget everything except her growing desire when she was with him. Simple things like the way he slipped his hand around her waist to guide her or his fondness for tucking strands of her hair behind her ear. The fleeting touches combined with the intensity of his gaze sometimes caught her off guard. He made her feel attractive and desirable, and she thrilled to the sizzle of their chemistry. He treated her as a woman he wanted to possess while reassuring her that he appreciated her intelligence and opinions.

"I thought the whole point of you dating him was so you could get in with the enemy."

"He never wants to discuss the oil rights," Chelsea told her sister. "I think we both recognize that we are on opposite sides of a fraught issue."

Her sister had driven a stake straight into the heart of Chelsea's dilemma. She had originally decided to go out with Nolan with the idea that she would dig for information. Instead, she'd avoided asking any questions that might disturb the positive energy flowing between them. Which meant she was doing exactly what her sister accused her of—she was dating the enemy and loving every second of it.

"Oh, for heaven's sake," Chelsea said, tossing her hands up in exasperation while her heart pounded erratically against her ribs. "It's been like a week and a half, and we've only gone out a few times." The actual number of official dates was six, but Chelsea kept that to herself. "It's going to take time to gain his trust."

"Time is of the essence," Layla reminded her.

"I know." Chelsea pinched the bridge of her nose to combat a growing headache. "I don't want them to ruin our ranch, but nothing is going to happen in the next few days."

Layla gave her a searching look. "This isn't like you."

"What isn't like me? I've never been one to rush into anything. I think everything through and then put a plan into place."

"Sure." Her sister sounded worried. "But you usually have a plan. I have not seen any sign of one. You are simply going out with that man and…" Layla cocked her head and studied Chelsea. "Enjoying him."

Chelsea made a strangled noise. "Don't be ridiculous."

"Deny it all you want, but I think you like him."

The only sound Chelsea could manage was some unimpressive sputtering. It was one thing to lie to her parents and Vic, but convincing Layla that she had everything under control was way harder.

"I do like him," Chelsea admitted and sighed. "He's been everywhere and has these amazing stories about all the things he's seen. Plus, he's easy on the eyes, and we've got great chemistry..."

"I knew it." With each syllable Chelsea had uttered, Layla's expression had grown more worried. "I just knew it. You are falling for him."

"*Falling* is a little extreme."

"You are falling for the guy. Why would you do that when you know the Thurstons can't be trusted?"

"I know they can't be trusted." Chelsea groaned softly. "Listen, I have everything under control. Honestly, when have you known me to do something rash?"

"You have always been the most sensible of any of us, and I know you're far more guarded since what happened with Brandon." Layla grew pensive. "But when it comes to love, none of us can see it coming."

Two months earlier, Layla had found love with Joshua, but a misguided ruse involving a twin switch nearly ruined their romance before it truly began.

"Whoa, no. Who said anything about love?" Chelsea waved her hands, desperate to ward off her sister's misguided assumptions. "There's no way I'm going there. I think he's hot as sin, and sure, I'm not going to deny that I wouldn't mind sleeping with him. But he's only in Royal temporarily. Eventually, he will have to get back to his globe-trotting ways. And my life is here. I'm not getting emotionally involved."

"I guess." Layla didn't seem all that convinced. "But I've seen you date other guys, and this is different. You're relaxed and seem really...secure."

Her sister's description made Chelsea flinch. Despite knowing their fling had an expiration date, she did feel secure with Nolan. Maybe because she had no possibility of a future with him, she could date him without expectations.

"I'm worried about you," Layla finished.

"You don't have to be. I just have a lot on my mind. Now that Grandpa is gone, Dad's timetable for choosing which of us will get control of the ranch has moved up. He's going to want to make sure his successor is thoroughly trained before he retires. Which means I have even less time to convince Dad that Vic doesn't deserve to be in charge. That's the only thing on my mind. Well, that and what might happen to the ranch if Heath succeeds in laying claim to the oil rights."

"Heath...? What about Nolan?" Layla never got her question answered, because Chelsea's phone began to ring.

When she glanced down and saw the caller was Nolan, her pulse jumped in anticipation of his whiskey-smooth voice in her ear.

"I have to take this." Chelsea stabbed her finger against the green button. Not until she spied her sister's astonished expression did she consider what her actions had revealed about her feelings for him.

"This is exactly what I'm talking about," Layla

protested, adding an exaggerated eye roll to further punctuate her disgust.

"Hey." Chelsea shot daggers at her sister before turning her back and striding the width of the house away from Layla. "What's up?"

"I just wanted to finalize our meeting time tomorrow."

She liked that he never left her hanging regarding plans. She'd dated guys in the past who left things until the last minute or never bothered to call when they were running late. To her mind, that was the height of rudeness. She knew that some men didn't communicate well, but what was the big deal about letting a girl know that you couldn't make a date? And then there was Brandon. She'd thought they were serious until one day he'd neglected to show up and then didn't respond to her texts or calls asking him what was going on.

"I'll be by your place around two o'clock."

"Can you give me a hint what we're doing?" he asked.

"Nope. It's your turn to be surprised."

"I guess I'll just have to be patient. And speaking of that, are you sure you can't come by tonight?"

A surge of heat coiled in her midsection. His voice had taken on a smoky tone that drove her mad with longing.

Chelsea glanced toward her sister and sighed with regret. "No. The whole family has gathered for Sunday night dinner, and there's no way I can sneak away."

Layla was gesturing toward the French doors that

led from the deck to the great room. Chelsea waved at her to go ahead. Instead, her sister stood beside the doors with her arms crossed, looking like she planned to scowl at Chelsea until she ended the call and came inside.

"Then I'll just have to wait and see you tomorrow."

"It'll be worth the wait, I promise."

"I'm counting on it. G'night, Ms. Dreamy. Sweet dreams." His warm goodbye sent pleasure spiraling through her.

"You, too."

It seemed hard to believe they'd only gone out a handful of times, and each time was more amazing than the last. Not that they'd all been as noteworthy as the gondola ride or dinner at Cocott, but Nolan was fun to be around and made even the most mundane activities a lot of fun.

If only she'd been able to find this sense of camaraderie in someone who wasn't trying to mess with her family's ranch. The unfairness of it all felt like being clocked in the jaw. For a brief second, her chest grew uncomfortably tight.

All too aware that her sister continued to radiate disapproval, Chelsea composed her face into bland disinterest and headed for the house. After one final look over and an *uh-huh* of disgust, Layla—and her opinions about Chelsea's feelings for Nolan—preceded her sister into the house.

To Chelsea's relief, Layla made no attempt to bring her concerns up to the family over dinner. This didn't mean that the conversation wasn't at the forefront of

Chelsea's mind. Was she too wrapped up in Nolan? Well, obviously, she found him handsome, charming and intriguing, but while every inch of him appealed to her, he was in league with his brother to ruin her family's ranch. That should bother her so much that she found Nolan detestable. Only she didn't.

The man had a body to die for and the engaging personality to match it. He made her laugh at a time when she was too stressed to even smile. She in turn made excuses for what he and Heath intended to do to her and to her family.

Why was she doing this to herself? Even without the feud between their families, it was never going to work between them. And yet she couldn't bring herself to stop seeing him. Despite knowing he would eventually run off in search of adventure. In spite of the worry that he could be using her to further his family's claim to what lay beneath her family's land.

Layla was right. Chelsea was becoming emotionally invested in Nolan. The game she was playing was a perilous one, because the person most in danger of getting fooled was her.

Seven

When Chelsea showed up at his door in tight jeans and a red crop top that bared her chiseled abdomen, Nolan had no idea how he was going to get them both out of the loft before he lost his battle with lust. The top was held together by a line of tiny strawberry buttons, and Nolan imagined he could hear them pinging off his walls as he tore it open. Did she have any idea how much he adored her in red? Before meeting her, his favorite color had been blue. Now he was obsessed with shades from crimson to scarlet, as long as they encased Chelsea's lean curves.

"I hope you're ready for anything," she said, her eyes glowing with excitement.

They'd been out to dinner several times when she could get away from the demands of the ranch for a few hours. Today, they had a longer date planned, an outing Chelsea insisted on keeping a surprise. Her saucy grin broadcast how much she liked being in control. In fact, Nolan enjoyed it as well.

Nolan raised an eyebrow as he gestured her inside. "I'm game if you are."

"I'm so game."

Not only was she a treat for the eyes, she smelled good enough to eat. Her shoulder brushed his chest as she passed by, and he caught a whiff of her berry-scented lotion. Suddenly besieged by the need to nibble his way up and down her fragrant skin, Nolan took in her playful updo and red lip as she sashayed into his living room. Her cowboy boots gave her hips a gentle rolling motion that seized his attention and wouldn't let go.

"You look great," he rasped, losing control of his voice.

"So do you." Her gaze held smoky approval as she took in his worn jeans and snug V-neck T-shirt. She reached out and picked up the medallion he wore around his neck, the light brush of her fingers singeing him through the thin fabric. "This is cool. Something you picked up on your travels?"

"Tibet. It's a Kalachakra, a powerful mantra for peace. It reduces suffering by calming negativity and conflict." He covered her hand with his so that they held the necklace together. "These represent the moon, the sun and the flame. It's a symbol of good fortune and protection for the wearer."

"All that sounds like something I could use." A

wistful sigh puffed from her lips. "Next time you're there, pick me up one, will you?"

"How about you just take the one I'm wearing?" He lifted the chain off his neck and dropped it over her head. The pendant settled amid the column of strawberry buttons between her breasts, and Nolan gave himself several seconds to admire the way the silver chain looked against her tan skin.

"Are you sure? It came all the way from Tibet. Are you sure you can part with it?" She turned her big brown eyes on him, and Nolan knew he'd give her this and more to make her happy.

"It looks like it was made for you."

"Thank you." Sending her fingers tunneling through his hair, she drew him down for a grateful kiss. She nipped at his lower lip before opening her mouth to the thrust of his tongue. Eager to take things further, he groaned as she eased away, whispering, "I'm going to treasure it."

With his hormones dancing in appreciation of her soft breasts grazing his chest, Nolan smiled down at her. Her lips remained softly parted, and Nolan knew if he kept staring at them, he'd claim her mouth all over again. He was close to surrendering to the urge to scoop her into his arms, carry her to bed and rip off every one of those strawberry buttons with his teeth. His fingers twitched as he imagined himself giving the top one a fierce twist. One by one, they would fall to the floor, exposing her beautiful breasts. He was mentally sliding his lips over one lush curve when the fingers gliding down his cheek fell away. The sudden loss knocked him out of his trance.

"Should we get going?" From her bright tone, Nolan suspected she had no sense of the fierce hunger raging inside him.

With the imprint of her final caress lingering on his skin, Nolan scrubbed his hand across his jaw and somehow summoned the strength to croak, "Sure."

If he didn't get them out of the condo, he would never know what surprises she'd organized for him. And from the gleeful anticipation sparkling in her gaze, she was looking forward to whatever she had planned.

Nolan watched her charming butt as she descended the stairs ahead of him. Damn. It was going to be a long afternoon.

Since Chelsea knew where they were going, she drove. Whatever she'd planned must've been a doozy, because she was bubbling with excitement. Nolan liked this take-charge side of her, mostly because reveling in her power made her that much more attractive. Her brown eyes glowed with satisfaction while a mysterious smile teased her lips. Her high spirits were infectious, and Nolan found his nerves humming as they traveled a series of two-lane roads.

"Almost there," she assured him, casting a teasing look his way. "You are going to be so surprised."

She turned off the highway onto a road that ran parallel to a well-maintained landing strip.

Mystified, he searched the small airfield. "Are we flying somewhere?"

"You might say that."

They flashed past a sign. "Skydiving?" The one-word question burst from him on a laugh. "This is what you want to do?"

"You're certified, and I called and confirmed that with your credentials we can jump tandem."

Nolan's entire body flushed with anticipation. She'd been intrigued when he talked about his experiences, but he'd never imagined she'd be interested in jumping herself.

"Are you sure about this?"

"Aren't you?"

"Of course. I've made nearly a hundred jumps…" He trailed off as she parked. "You trust me to keep you safe?"

It wasn't just the jump he was asking about.

Flashing her even, white teeth, Chelsea shut off the engine and turned to face him. "There's no one I'd rather jump out of a plane strapped to."

Nolan slid his fingers into her thick hair and tugged to draw her closer. "You, Ms. Dreamy, continue to bewitch and amaze me."

"I'm glad." Her lashes fanned her cheeks as his head dipped and their lips grew steadily closer. "With everything you've seen and done, I wasn't sure I could find something adventurous enough for you."

He dusted soft kisses across her lips, mingling their breath. "If you're doing this for me, it's not necessary. Being with you is adventure enough for me."

"That's sweet." While her fingertips traced a line of fire down his neck, she nipped his jawline and then lightly raked his earlobe with her teeth. "But being with you has inspired me to be a little reckless, and I want to test the mettle of my bravery."

Nolan shuddered as his nerves went incandescent in response to her tantalizing touch. "I've been trying like hell not to ravish you these last few days, but I can't promise to be good after jumping out of an airplane with you strapped to my body."

"The anticipation has been killing me, too," she whispered, her eyes blazing with hunger. She took his hand and placed his palm over her breast, then moaned as his fingers kneaded gently.

For the last week, he'd been reminding himself that anticipation could heighten pleasure. When he at last slept with Chelsea, he intended the moment be absolutely memorable. For both of them. But he was near the end of his rope, and skydiving with her was sure to push him beyond the limits of his control.

"We could just go park somewhere deserted and take the edge off." His fingers roamed over her abs and teased the waistband of her jeans. She rotated her hips in his direction and slid her foot over his leg. The console between them was a problem.

"I think about you at night," she whispered, her voice fierce and urgent as her tongue flicked against his neck. "I imagine you doing all kinds of things to me."

The sexy words made him desperate for her. "Do you come when you think of what I'm doing?"

He dipped his hand between her legs. She gasped as he stroked her sensitive flesh, the heat of her no less tantalizing for it being muffled by the fabric of her jeans. They both panted as she rocked against his palm. Nolan sent his lips roaming down the delicate column of her neck. When he reached the spot where her shoulder started, he eased the edges of his teeth into her skin, gently but with enough pressure to leave the tiniest of marks.

"Yes," she moaned on the thinnest whisper of air, and even more softly she added, "Again."

As he gave her what she wanted, Nolan found himself spiraling into another reality, a sensual, intoxicating realm that existed for just the two of them.

Nolan dimly noticed the sound of a car door slamming, and a second later he was jerked back into awareness of their surroundings by the staccato blast of a horn as someone locked their vehicle. He set his forehead against hers, all too conscious of his ragged breathing and unsteady pulse. They sat that way for a long time while their bodies calmed. But even as his heart rate steadied, his need for her continued to smolder.

"Being with you is all the rush I need," he told her, wondering how she'd feel about him after jumping out of a plane at ten thousand feet.

"That's music to my ears." She dropped a brief kiss on his lips. "Now, let's go skydiving."

Chelsea barely felt the impact as she and Nolan landed in the empty field that had been designated as the landing site. Her entire body was lit up with adrenaline and desire. The jump had been spectacular, a breath-stealing plunge through the heavens, followed by a leisurely drift along the thermals after the chute had bloomed above them. For someone who normally kept her feet firmly planted on the ground, the experience had electrified her. And left her pondering all she'd given up by choosing to focus her energy on the ranch.

"That was crazy," she yelled as Nolan released her harness from his. "Amazing."

Robbed of his strong, reassuring presence behind her, Chelsea stumbled and would've fallen, except he caught her and spun her into his arms. Her heart fluttered wildly at the intensity of his expression as his arm wrapped around her, squeezing her against him once more. Before she had a chance to say a word, his lips crashed down on hers. Wild, intoxicating emotion exploded through her, and she pushed into the kiss, wrapping her arms around his neck and feasting on his mouth.

He lifted her off the ground, and she wrapped her thighs around his waist. Her arms encircled his shoulders as the press of his erection against the most sensitive parts sent her body into spasms of joy. She wiggled her hips, driving her heated core against him. Nolan dropped to his knees and, with his arm binding Chelsea to his chest, lowered her to the cushion of grass in the big, empty field.

His lips coasted down her throat. She cupped his head and arched her back, offering him more of her skin to nibble on. The heat of the July afternoon was unbearable, but it was nothing compared to the inferno raging inside her. Chelsea squirmed in an effort to free herself from the binding harness, and sensing her distress, Nolan rolled them until he lay beneath her.

With a triumphant gasp, Chelsea sat up, popped the catch in the middle of her chest and ripped the straps off her shoulders. Panting, she attacked Nolan's clasp. His fingers curved over her bare waist between the crop top and her jeans, thumbs riding the ripple of her ribs, making her hands shake as she struggled to get her hands on his skin in turn. Seconds later, she let out a satisfied sigh as she successfully tunneled her fingers beneath the hem of his shirt and rode his six-pack to his impressive pecs. As he groaned in pleasure, she curved her fingers and lightly raked her nails across his nipples. She grinned as a sharp expletive escaped his parted lips.

"I want you, right here, right now," she told him, leaning down to seize his lower lip between her teeth.

"You're killing me, you know that, right?"

"I'm glad." She didn't mean to come off all cocky and was glad to see he didn't take her words at face value. His crooked smile gave her a second to gather her wits. "What I mean is every time you touch me, I go wild, and I'm really glad I can do the same for you."

"Trust me, you do."

Nolan lifted his hips and drove his erection against her tender flesh. She met his thrust with a little twist of her own that made them both moan with frustration and pleasure.

"As hot as it would be to do this here and now," he said, "we really are not gonna have time to do it right before we're picked up." Yet even as he said this, he sank his long fingers into her hair and pulled her close for a sizzling kiss. After a long time, he released her lips and murmured, "And I want all the time in the world to make love to you."

Chelsea shuddered at his declaration and recognized that he was right. As hungry as she was for him, a frantic coupling in a field was not how she wanted their first time together to happen.

"So, back to your place right now, or dinner first?" She'd planned for the latter, but with desire raging through her veins, she wasn't sure she could eat anything. Not while she was starved for the six feet of sizzling male who'd slid his fingers beneath her crop top and cupped her lace-covered breasts.

"Definitely dinner," he teased, whisking his thumbs over her nipples. "I want the anticipation to build."

"You don't think it's been building?" she asked, finishing with a little gasp as he nibbled on her ear.

"It has for me from the moment I set eyes on you across Main Street."

His admission sent a familiar thrill up her spine. She wasn't used to having a man seduce her with words. She'd always been so practical with those she chose to date in the past.

"Please, can we just go back to your place?" She made the request in a small, breathless voice, unaccustomed to begging for what she wanted. "I can't wait any longer to be with you."

"I'd like that more than anything."

As more kisses followed, each one hotter and deeper, Chelsea wondered if he had any idea that she'd shared more with him than with any man she'd ever known.

She'd confided how her father's lack of faith in her abilities saddened her. Voiced the question if Vic became the sibling in charge, what that meant for her future. Most days she got up and applied a tough persona along with her mascara and lipstick. None of her family knew about Chelsea's deep anxiety, but she'd drawn back the curtain and put her fragile confidence on display for Nolan.

It should terrify her that she'd revealed her insecurity. Yet maintaining her defenses with Nolan hadn't seemed necessary. He'd given her a safe space to explore her fears because he'd been willing to share his concerns about his relationship with his brother, the pain of losing his mother and sister and his regret that staying away these last fifteen years had robbed him of precious time with them.

They were oblivious to the vehicle that rolled up on them until the light tap of a horn roused them from their sex-fogged delirium. Chelsea and Nolan jerked apart, laughing as they resettled their clothes and got to their feet. Another time, a different man, and Chelsea would've been mortified to be caught making out in public, but being with Nolan was so easy and fun that she didn't mind the knowing looks cast her way by the driver and his passengers.

Hand in hand, she and Nolan headed to the van.

They settled into the back and grinned at each other in delight, but the intense gleam in his eyes made Chelsea uncomfortably aware of the throbbing heat between her thighs. How was she supposed to survive the hour-long drive back to Royal? Anticipation, hell. She was in serious distress.

"Let's get out of here," Nolan whispered in her ear once they were back at the skydiving base. He slid his hand into the back pocket of her jeans and gave a little squeeze. "I need to be inside you before I lose my mind."

His sexy words made her breath hitch. "I want that, too." She handed him her keys. "Feel like driving? I don't feel all that steady at the moment."

Taking the keys, he planted a quick, hard kiss on her lips before nudging her toward the passenger side of the truck. If the drive back to Royal seemed to take forever, at least she was lost in a blissful daze. She distantly heard herself asking Nolan about his other skydiving adventures and tried to pay attention to his answers, but with her blood pounding hot and fierce through her veins, she struggled to concentrate on anything but what would happen when they returned to his loft.

They barely made it through the door before Chelsea launched herself at him. She dived her fingers into his lush, wavy hair and reached up on tiptoe to press her mouth to his. The kiss started hot and hungry but quickly slowed down as Nolan gently caressed her burning cheek and ran his tongue along her bottom lip. A breath eased out of her tight chest as he played with her lips, pressing and nibbling kisses that were both tender and hungry.

Instead of moving them to his waiting bed, Nolan picked her up and set her on the nearby kitchen counter.

"Here?" she squeaked, losing control of her voice as he stepped between her parted thighs and ground his erection into her.

"For a start."

Eyes glowing with wicked intent, he gripped her boot and slid it off her foot. She barely heard the bang as it hit the wood floor above the pounding of her heart. While he loosened the second boot, she shimmied out of the crop top, letting it fall. His eyes lit with approval as he scanned her pale breasts encased in red lace.

"Damn," he murmured. "I do love you in red."

She reached behind her for the clasp. "How do you feel about me out of it?" In seconds the bra had come undone, and his gaze found hers as he peeled the straps down her arm, exposing her.

"You are perfection," he murmured, his lips easing onto the delicate skin behind her ear, making her quiver.

His palm pressed hard between her thighs, inviting her to rub her tender parts against him. In a rising frenzy of desire, she realized how close she was to coming.

"Nolan," she panted. "This is… You are… I'm…" She fumbled with the zipper on her jeans, needing his fingers inside her. Before she'd done more than popped the button, an orgasm broke over her like a wave, shattering her into pieces. "Damn." Part relief, part protest, the curse made him chuckle.

"Most women enjoy coming," he muttered before his mouth clamped down over hers. He drove his tongue forward to tangle with hers, and she half sobbed as aftershocks pummeled her.

Her release was only partially satisfying. What she truly craved was his possession. To be filled by him and made whole. And Nolan seemed to understand, because he finished stripping off her jeans and underwear, hooked his fingers in the waistband and tugged the denim off her hips and down her legs.

A startled laugh escaped as her naked butt connected with the cool stone countertop, but then his hand found the heat between her legs and she went up in flames.

"You're so wet," he said, sliding his fingers across her.

A greedy moan poured from her lips. "That feels so good. I've been waiting so long..." She captured his face in hers and kissed him hard. "You know what would feel better, though? If you got naked, too, and we went over to that big bed of yours. I need your skin against mine." Their hearts beating together.

That last bit was too romantic to say out loud. As much as she might enjoy talking dirty in bed, she was terrified to send him running by divulging that her need for him was more than physical.

Nolan bracketed her hips in his strong fingers and lowered his forehead to hers. "I want that, too."

She reached between them to unfasten his jeans and worked feverishly until she had them off his hips. Hissing in appreciation at the impressive tent his erection made in his boxer briefs, she carefully released it from the confining fabric. He set his head against her shoulder and shuddered as her hand closed around him.

A curse slipped from his lips as she explored his hard length, learning its velvety surface and the shape beneath. All too soon he covered her hand with his and pulled it away from him.

"No more." He lifted her palm to his lips, nibbling on the sensitive mound near her thumb. "There's only so much willpower available when I'm with you."

"I don't want you to hold back."

He snorted. "Ms. Dreamy, I'm just trying to hold on."

And then he was stepping out of his jeans, ripping his T-shirt over his head. She barely got a chance to appreciate the impressive cut of his biceps, the rolling muscles of his shoulders or the toned beauty of his abs before he slid his hands beneath her butt cheeks and lifted her. With a surprised murmur, she wrapped her arms and legs around him as he carried her—at long last—to his bed.

Eight

Nolan set Chelsea down on her feet beside his bed and took a step back, astonished at his rapid heart rate and the irregular cadence of his breathing. "Let me look at you," he said, his eyes roving over her naked perfection, seeing the effort it cost her to hold still beneath his scrutiny. "You are gorgeous."

"You're not so bad yourself."

"I can't wait to get to know every inch of you."

"I want that." She blew out a ragged breath. "Can we get started?"

"You're in a hurry?"

"I'm suddenly really nervous."

This was his moment to reassure her, so Nolan stepped closer and cupped her cheek in one palm. "You don't need to be nervous. I'll take care of you."

He threaded her long hair through his fingers and gave a gentle tug.

"I know you will," she responded, edging closer until the heat of their skin leaped across the narrow distance between them and burned away her hesitation. She smoothed her hand over his chest, fingers dancing over his pecs. "In fact, I'm counting on it."

Nolan drew in a deep breath and sighed as she raked her nails down his abs, letting her nerves settle as she explored his hard planes, the structure of bones beneath his overheated skin. At last he could take no more and took her by the shoulders, pivoting her toward the bed. As the backs of her knees encountered the mattress, she flopped backward, spreading her arms wide as she landed. Nolan stared hungrily at her firm breasts, watching her nipples harden beneath his regard. Shooting him an enticing grin, she wiggled her way toward the middle of the bed.

Reaching into the nightstand, he pulled out a condom and slid it on. Her eyes flashed, feral and wild, as she watched his every movement.

"Nolan." Greedy and impatient, his name was a growl torn from her lips. She arched her back and drew her fingertips from her navel to the cleft between her breasts. "Touch me, please."

He smiled wolfishly. Setting his knee on the bed beside her, he caressed along her thigh and into the indent of her waist, riding her ribs to the soft curve of her breast. She sucked in a breath as he cupped her gently and then squeezed before feathering fingertips across her tight nipples.

"This is where I've wanted you from the first moment I saw you," he murmured, his voice hot and hungry. Nolan captured one rosy bud between his lips and flicked his tongue over it. "Naked, in my bed."

"I want you," she whispered, her thighs falling open as she rocked her hips. "Make me yours."

Her plea lanced through him like lightning. It felt so good to have her hands roaming over his body, but he'd waited so long to have her, and holding back much longer might have catastrophic consequences. He shifted between her thighs, settling his hand on the back of her leg, opening her wide, making room for himself. She obliged with a soft purr of delight, raking her fingers through his hair.

He took his erection in one hand and teased her with the head, coating himself in her wet heat. She gasped as he sank into her, and he stilled.

"Does it hurt?"

She shook her head. "You feel amazing. More. I want all of you."

"I can give you more." He circled her thigh with his fingers and hitched it over his hip, opening her up so he could go deeper.

"Yes." She gave a breathless nod and sank her fingers into his forearm as he pulled back and stroked forward once again. "Like that."

This time, as he lay fully embedded in her, he brought his hand to her face and dragged his thumb over her soft lips. He'd never felt this closeness with anyone before and knew she'd gifted him with a glimpse into the tender emotions she kept hidden.

"You're incredible."

Her lashes fluttered. "You make me feel that way."

And then desire took over and Nolan had to move. He kept his strokes smooth and rhythmic, watching her reaction to each thrust. A delectable smile curved her soft lips, and she lost herself in their lovemaking. Watching her, Nolan found his own grin forming. What was it about her?

"Harder," she commanded.

With a reverent groan, he obliged, pumping faster, harder, aware that she was dissolving beneath him, her cries growing more reckless and abandoned. Panting as he surged toward the threshold of ecstasy, Nolan had just enough presence of mind to make sure Chelsea came with him.

"Come for me," he coaxed, each second carrying him nearer his climax. He loved how the world had fallen away and there was only Chelsea.

She wrapped her legs around him tighter, signaling she was close to the edge as well. Nolan watched her, waiting for the telltale signs, feeling her body quickening as his own screamed at him to let go. And then she was there, her body bucking with the power of it, her inner muscles contracting on him, drawing him deep and hard into her as an orgasm tore through her like a tornado. Nolan took it all in for several heartbeats, watched her shatter and then let himself be pulled apart in her arms.

In the aftermath, Nolan's lips drifted along her damp skin, smiling at the salty taste of her, breathing in the sexy musk of her arousal. He wanted to know all her scents and sounds and flavors. To hear her snore softly in her sleep and press her round backside against his morning erection. So much to learn. Yet he couldn't help but hear a ticking clock in the background. A warning that stolen moments like these wouldn't last forever.

"You know, I could get used to this," she murmured, nuzzling into his throat, her teeth nipping suggestively. She'd draped her arms over his shoulders, and despite her boneless lassitude, he could tell her thoughts were spinning. "Let's stay in bed like this forever."

As Nolan processed her statement, a wave of goose bumps rushed over his skin. Little by little she was shedding all the protective layers she wore to keep herself safe. Originally, he'd thought he could romance her, get the information Heath needed and move on. Assuming what was between them was strictly physical, he'd stupidly believed that afterward, he could walk away. But each hour in her company had brought him to a new level of understanding, of appreciation.

"I wouldn't mind that." His palms glided over her silken curves, noting the hard muscle beneath.

Her body was the exact opposite of her personality. She presented the world with this fierce toughness, while inside she was tender and vulnerable. No doubt most people believed she was hard as nails. It's probably why she got hurt over and over. This was how she'd allowed herself to be misunderstood in the past. She'd fallen for men who never saw or couldn't appreciate the fragility hidden beneath her thick skin.

"But of course, that's truly unrealistic," she went on as if he hadn't spoken. Her breath puffed against his skin as she sighed. "I mean, I can't let myself get used to this, because I don't know how long you're going to be around."

Nolan's gut clenched as he heard the resignation in her voice at their inevitable separation. "I haven't really decided what I'm gonna do," he said, which was the first time he'd voiced his inner turmoil out loud.

"You don't expect me to believe that you'd consider staying in Royal. Not after being gone for fifteen years. Your business involves location scouting around the world."

He'd known she was too shrewd to believe such a glib response. "Being back here has been nice." Claiming he'd had a change of heart and intended to stick around might've worked on another woman, but not Chelsea. Still, that didn't stop him from trying. "I've enjoyed reconnecting with my brother, and meeting you has given me food for thought."

She set her chin on his chest and hit him with a solemn gaze. "I don't believe you."

Her declaration really did give him food for thought. She'd been burned so often that winning her trust might be nearly impossible. And he wanted her to believe him. Not to help with his brother's plan regarding the oil rights, but because each glimpse past her shields had touched his heart. It made him want to enclose her in Bubble Wrap and take care of her, even as she claimed she needed no one's help. He'd never put another person's welfare before his own, and the change in his perspective rattled him.

"You don't believe people can change their minds about things?" he asked.

"I'd be every kind of fool to be that pessimistic when I am doing everything in my power to change my dad's mind about letting me be in charge of the ranch." She rolled her head to the side so that her ear rested over his steadily beating heart. "Yet there's a big part of me that doubts I'll be successful."

Her expression grew so pensive that Nolan decided she was unaccustomed to coming clean about her own inner demons. His gut tightened. That she'd trusted him with something so private warned him to tread carefully.

"I've learned that getting what you want often involves making compromises. Sometimes when I find a perfect place to shoot, convincing the owners to let us disrupt their property for several months means we have to find some way to make it worth their while. Maybe it's as simple as writing a big check. Sometimes they want to be a part of the action."

"Are you saying I'm wrong for wanting it all?"

"Never. I'm just saying that sometimes what you think you want isn't what you need. Like, our budget was super tight on one shoot and we found the perfect spot, but the property owner asked five grand for two weeks. He was an aspiring songwriter, so instead of paying him the money he wanted, we arranged for him to write one of the songs on the soundtrack."

"What I want is to run the ranch." She paused, and her eyebrow quirked in challenge. "What do you think I need?"

"Me."

"Hello, stranger," Natalie teased, but her tone wasn't at all lighthearted as she slid into the booth opposite Chelsea.

The women had decided to meet for lunch at the Royal Diner, a popular eatery in downtown that was decorated like an old-fashioned 1950s diner with red faux-leather booths and black-and-white-checkered floors, where owner Amanda Battle served classic diner meals.

"What do you mean, stranger?" Chelsea protested, her enthusiasm for this lunch with her best friend dimming. "I saw you just the other day. We went shopping, remember?"

"For an outfit you could wear on your next date with Nolan."

"I thought we had fun trying stuff on. I didn't realize... I mean, does it bother you that I'm dating him? You were the one who suggested he was interested in me in the first place."

"I know." Natalie made a face. "I thought you'd have some fun with him and loosen up a bit. All you've done for months is obsess about your dad picking Vic to run the ranch. But it just seems like you've traded one obsession for another."

Chelsea's mood dipped still further. She was tired of everybody harassing her about Nolan. Why couldn't her family and friends just accept that she knew what she was doing?

"Don't you realize that the two things are connected? If I can convince Nolan that he and Heath shouldn't pursue the oil rights, then I will have saved the ranch and my dad will have to put me in charge."

"I know." Natalie frowned. "It's just that ever since you and Nolan started getting serious—"

"Serious?" Chelsea interrupted, panic stirring as she contemplated Natalie's take on what was happening between her and Nolan. "We aren't serious. I mean, we've only been going out for a couple of weeks."

"A couple of weeks where I've never seen you so preoccupied. Not even after Brandon ghosted you right before you were supposed to meet his parents." Natalie paused and frowned at her. "You've changed a bunch since you've started seeing him."

Chelsea considered the way Nolan brought out her adventurous side. "Maybe I needed to change a little. I mean, for years people have been telling me to lighten up and have some fun. Why is it the minute I start taking that advice, you all get on my case for it?"

"I don't think anybody begrudges you some fun." Natalie looked uncomfortable. "I just wonder if you should be having fun with Nolan Thurston. You are moving really fast."

"Fast?"

She thought about her friends from college who jumped into bed with a guy on the first date. At least she'd waited until the seventh date to sleep with

Nolan. Okay, so it was fast for her. She'd dated her last boyfriend for three months before taking things into the bedroom. And look how that one had turned out. Brandon had been the perfect guy on paper. Well educated. A great job. Sophisticated. They'd gone to the best restaurants. Attended concerts and the theater. Things had been going great until they slept together. And then, after arranging for them to have dinner with his parents, he'd just vanished.

"Yes, fast."

"Well, maybe it is." Chelsea reflected on the last two weeks. "The fact is, I like him, and he makes me feel things I've never known before."

She'd never connected with anyone this fast or with this level of confidence. Natalie might think Chelsea had fallen hard for Brandon, but in fact, she'd turned a blind eye to many warning signs. Nolan aroused no such misgivings. Well, except for his part in claiming the oil rights beneath the Grandin ranch.

"And that's my point," Natalie continued, oblivious to her friend's turmoil. "You usually start dating a guy armed with a checklist and a clear idea of the sort of future you could have with him. Have you considered just how complicated any sort of relationship with Nolan would be? He and his brother are coming after the oil beneath your land."

"And I'm hoping that I can change his mind about that."

"Have you considered that maybe he's hoping to get you on his side?" Natalie's look of utter pity shoved Chelsea hard against the back of the booth.

"He's not." But her claim lacked conviction.

"You don't know that. You don't know anything about him." Natalie sighed in exasperation. "It's crazy that you are throwing yourself into a relationship with him when you have no idea what tricks he has up his sleeve."

Was she misreading Nolan's signals?

"First of all, we're not in a relationship. You don't think I realize that he's not going to settle down in Royal?" Chelsea's throat tightened. She had grown accustomed to Nolan and hated contemplating the day when he'd have to go. But she wasn't unrealistic about it. For the moment, she just wanted to enjoy their time together. And having everyone throwing their suspicions in her face was making that damned hard. "Maybe he is using me. Maybe I'm using him. It's not like I'm clueless. Maybe I'm not being my normal sensible self, but I'm sick of playing it safe. It hasn't gotten me anywhere, and I like the way Nolan makes me feel."

Natalie shook her head. "I just think you're asking for trouble."

"A little trouble is what I need at the moment." Before Nolan came along, she'd been making herself miserable fighting an upward battle against her family's patriarchal leanings. What if after all her hard work, Vic ended up in charge and she'd never taken the time to ride on a gondola or jump out of an airplane? "What's so great about playing it safe?"

"You don't get hurt." Natalie's voice had taken on a hollow tone.

"But you don't have any fun, either." Chelsea leaned her arms on the table and pinned Natalie with her gaze. "Maybe you need to take a risk. Why not jump-start your own social life with somebody interesting?"

"Interesting like who?"

"Jonathan Lattimore comes to mind," Chelsea said, paying close attention to her friend's reaction. "You've had a crush on him for a long time. Why don't you make the first move?"

The Lattimore family owned the ranch next door to the Grandins. Victor Sr. and Augustus Lattimore had been best friends. Like Chelsea, Jonathan was the oldest child of their generation. The families had a warm relationship—so much so that both sides had hoped Jonathan would marry either Chelsea or Layla, but the trio had never been anything but good friends.

Although Natalie hid it well, Chelsea knew her friend well enough to recognize that she had a crush on the eldest Lattimore son. It had often surprised Chelsea that her confident, beautiful friend had never let Jonathan know she was interested in him. Maybe she hadn't had the courage to do so before Jonathan got married, but now that he was divorced, Natalie still hadn't made her feelings known.

"I don't want to talk about Jonathan," Natalie grumbled. She picked up her menu and deliberately stopped talking.

"Oh, so you can badger me about Nolan, but I make one comment about you asking Jonathan out and that's the end of the conversation?"

"Jonathan isn't interested in me." Natalie was

sounding as annoyed as Chelsea had felt moments earlier. "Nothing could ever happen between us."

In Chelsea's opinion, Jonathan had been so devastated by his failed marriage that he'd closed himself off. "Maybe he'd be interested in you if he had some inkling you had a crush on him."

Natalie looked aghast. "I can't let him know I'm attracted to him. What if he's not interested and it gets awkward between us?"

"You don't think it's awkward between you now? Well, maybe not on his part, because he has no clue how you feel." Chelsea wished her stunning, talented best friend had half the confidence when it came to romance that she demonstrated in her career. "But I've seen you when he comes into the room—you get completely tongue-tied."

"I know what you're doing. You're trying to distract me from warning you about Nolan."

Chelsea sighed. "Not at all. I am simply trying to point out that taking a risk with your heart might be better for you than you think."

"You are falling for Nolan Thurston, aren't you?"

"I don't know if I'd say I am falling for him," Chelsea demurred. "I know that we don't have a future. He will eventually return to his international travels, and I will remain in Royal and hopefully be running Grandin Ranch. No matter what happens, I will always cherish this time with him."

Chelsea was proud of herself. She sounded so practical and matter-of-fact, just the way she approached everything in her life. But thinking about the day when Nolan would leave tore her up inside. The old Chelsea would've stopped herself from becoming invested long before her heart had gotten engaged. But getting to know Nolan had changed her, opened her to joy and optimism. Her spirit soared in his company. His passion for adventure had awakened something exhilarating and irrepressible inside her.

There were moments she could actually imagine herself traveling with him to all the exotic places he visited in search of film locations. Of course, she would never want to experience the rough conditions he had told her about, but she could imagine herself on safari in South Africa or riding an elephant in Indonesia or camels in the Moroccan desert.

"Maybe that's the secret," Natalie murmured.

"The secret to what?"

"You're happy dating Nolan because there's no pressure from expectations. You recognize that eventually you'll both go your own ways, not because of some dramatic breakup, but because your lifestyles are incompatible."

Chelsea was glad she hadn't confessed to Natalie about the tiny seedling that had taken root in her subconscious. If her dad put Vic in charge, Chelsea might not end things with Nolan. She'd be in for even more lecturing if anyone got wind of that.

"I think the secret," Chelsea continued, "is to recognize what makes you happy and go after it."

Nine

Nolan was alone in the living room of the house he'd grown up in, talking on the phone to Chelsea. He'd agreed to have dinner with Heath but planned on joining Chelsea at his place later for dessert. They'd been together every night this week, but tonight was different—she was staying over for the first time. Since it was Friday night, she had the weekend free and was planning to spend her time off with him. The sleepover marked another stage in their relationship, and Nolan was surprised how smoothly things were progressing between them.

"Looking forward to seeing you later," he murmured into his phone, unable to resist a smile as he added in sultry tones, "And, of course, I mean *all* of you."

"The feeling is mutual," Chelsea replied in the throaty purr that drove him wild. "Eight o'clock. Don't be late."

She often said things like that, a holdover from other men she'd dated, who'd disappointed her by either being late all the time or not showing up at all. Nolan recognized it as a defense mechanism turned habit and promised he'd never give her a reason to doubt him.

"I won't."

The more time he spent in Chelsea's company, the harder it was to imagine any man standing her up. When they were apart, his thoughts were filled with her. No woman had ever appealed to him more. Her combination of intelligence, practicality and directness kept him on his toes, and their sexual chemistry was off the charts, leaving no doubt in his mind that she was as into him as he was into her.

In fact, the only negative thing about dating her had to do with her family and his being on opposite sides of the oil rights claim.

"You're seeing Chelsea again?" Heath asked, carrying two beers into the room and extending one to Nolan. He'd been in the middle of his own phone call when Nolan had arrived a few minutes earlier, a quick update from the lawyer, from what he'd overheard.

"Later tonight."

"Are you making any headway?" Heath's closed body language and the way he asked the question suggested he already knew Nolan was no longer on task.

He wasn't wrong.

As much as Nolan wanted to be on Heath's side, he could also sympathize with how afraid Chelsea was of what might happen to her family's ranch if Heath granted the rights to an oil company. That company would then be able to use the surface above the oil deposit as "reasonably necessary," and it was legally murky what that meant. After yesterday, when Chelsea had shown him a photo of her horse on her phone and told him all the things she loved about the ranch, he'd done some research and discovered that an oil company that leased the mineral rights could enter the property, build roads, use caliche found on the leased property, install pipelines to transport products from the lease, store equipment and inject salt water in disposal wells. Further, unless provisions were spelled out in the contract, an oil company could select the locations of wells and pipelines to be placed on the property without input from the surface owner.

The amount of destruction that could happen if Heath leased the rights to an oil company could devastate the Grandin and neighboring Lattimore ranches.

"I don't know if I'm making the sort of progress you'd be interested in." Picturing Chelsea as she'd looked the night before in his bed, Nolan sighed.

"You're sleeping with her." A declaration rather than a question, and one wrapped up in concern. "I suppose she's trying to win you over to her side."

"She's told me a few things about the ranch, and we've talked about the repercussions of having an oil company drilling on the land."

"I should've talked you out of getting to know her when you first spotted her on July Fourth." Heath looked grim as he studied his brother's face. "I was wrong to think you and I were on the same page."

The last thing Nolan wanted to do was disappoint his brother, but after Chelsea had explained the potential devastation to her ranch, he was no longer as committed to his brother's plan. Nor could he imagine a choice that would make them both happy.

This was the sort of conflict he usually avoided in his private life. Was it any wonder that he rarely stayed still long enough for trouble of a personal nature to manifest?

With his profession running him all over the world, he rarely formed attachments with women. He could keep up with his friends via text and video calls, but romantic relationships required him to be present in a way his business didn't permit.

Chelsea was different. With each day that passed, he was more consumed with wanting to be with her. To make love to her every day and sleep with her in his arms every night. Being away from her brought him physical pain and emotional distress. She was on his mind nonstop. He constantly caught himself wanting to send her links to interesting stories or ridiculous memes that he hoped would make her laugh.

"From the research I've done, it's bound to disrupt their operations and do permanent damage to their land," Nolan argued. "It just seems like there's enough destruction in the world." In the fifteen years he'd roamed the globe, Nolan had witnessed the slow-moving devastation that mankind was doing to the planet in the name of progress and capitalism.

"I really thought you were on my side."

"I am on your side," Nolan insisted, starting to realize that as long as he was involved with Chelsea, Heath would never believe him. "It's just that I have concerns."

Tension invaded Heath's body with each word Nolan uttered. The last thing Nolan wanted to do was worsen his relationship with his brother, but he couldn't turn his back on what was best for Chelsea and her family, either. Trapped as he was between a rock and a hard place, Nolan suspected if his feelings for Chelsea continued to grow, he would be forced to make a devastating choice.

"Have you wondered why Mom didn't assert her claim all these years?" Nolan asked. Was she too proud to take anything from Victor Grandin? Had Ladd Thurston known about the oil claim? Or had the couple decided that exercising the rights would've been more hassle than it was worth? "I mean, there were some lean years when the money would've been helpful."

"We'll never know why Mom stuffed the document in a drawer and never did anything about it." Heath's brown eyes hardened into smoky quartz. "Maybe she was bullied and afraid to take action."

Given the way the families were fighting against Heath, Nolan could see where the scenario played into his brother's narrative about why they should

treat the Grandins and Lattimores as their enemies.
Which didn't help Nolan's quandary. The thought of
having to battle with Chelsea's family made Nolan's
stomach twist. He didn't want to be stuck in the middle of a bitter fight.

"Or she didn't want to take anything from the
Grandins," Nolan pointed out, hoping his brother
might see the logic of this.

"I know there's no hard proof that Daniel Grandin
was Ashley's father," Heath said, restating the prem-
ise that motivated his action. "But Mom's papers, and
the fact that Victor Grandin gave her the oil rights,
point to it."

On that they both agreed. Yet the circumstances
that had led to the creation of the legal document
were less clear.

"While all that's true, both Mom and Ashley are
gone…"

Nolan couldn't imagine how awful the loss of their
mother and sister had been for Heath. Even though
Nolan hadn't been home for years, their loss had hit
him hard. But Heath's grief had taken him to a very
dark place. In the grip of strong emotions, when it
came to the oil rights, there was no reasoning with
him. Yet Nolan was determined to try.

"And I, for one, don't need the money." Nolan
braced himself for the next part. "I'm loath to do
harm just so we can become wealthier."

"I'm not doing this for us." Heath looked disappointed by Nolan's assumption.

"You're not?"

"No. All this is for Ashley. She started a foundation but died before getting it off the ground. The money will fund her legacy."

"Oh, wow!" The knot in Nolan's chest began to ease as Heath went on to explain Ashley's vision for the foundation.

Heath's explanation shone a whole new light on his obsession. Two years ago, after burying their mother and sister, the brothers had talked long into the night about their mutual loss. Sadly, their shared grief hadn't been enough to bridge the chasm between them created by misunderstanding, resentment and distance. Now Nolan wondered if he'd done even more damage by misreading Heath's motivation.

Yet he couldn't be sure if that's all there was to his brother's crusade. If all Heath wanted was to ensure Ashley's foundation lived on, then why hadn't he come out and said this earlier? Nolan wondered if Heath knew perfectly well the destruction an oil company could do and wanted to hurt the Grandins. It worried Nolan that Heath might have lost his way.

"I want to do right by our sister," Nolan said. "And I know it's important to you that she live on through the foundation, but is it worth destroying someone else's dream in the process?"

"You mean Chelsea's dream?"

The accusation hit home, but Nolan pictured her beautiful face and worried brown eyes, his resolve hardening. "She's just trying to save her family's ranch."

"You realize that both sides can't win." Heath looked unconcerned by his brother's dilemma.

"Yeah, I guess I do."

Chelsea lay on her stomach, legs bent, feet in the air while she flipped through the Sunday paper. Beside her on the king-size bed, Nolan drank coffee and read the sports section. He wore only a pair of boxers, and Chelsea had a hard time focusing on the headlines.

"You know," she said, giving up trying to read and ogling Nolan from beneath her lashes. She adored all his rippling muscles and bronze skin. Nibbling on her lower lip, she pondered how wonderful it had been to wake up snuggled against him that morning and savor his fingertips roving over her curves. "Of all the things we've done these last few weeks, I think this is my favorite."

"Personally, I liked the cowgirl museum." Nolan looked absolutely serious. "It gave me a much greater appreciation of all the contributions the women of Texas have made."

If another man had said this, Chelsea might take it as sarcasm, but Nolan had shown such a genuine interest in all the exhibits. In fact, the entire time she'd known him, every reaction he displayed rang true. It was refreshing to date someone and not have to speculate where his head was. If she wanted to know his opinion, all she had to do was ask. He would give her insight into what was on his mind.

"That was nice, but I'm happiest when we're hanging out. Like this." She gestured with her hand to indicate the bed. "I hope we get a lot more weekends like this." She noted his fleeting frown, and doubt crept in. "I suppose that's not likely to happen. You are probably going to be contacted about a project anytime now." He'd mentioned that several of the production studios he'd worked with in the past were in the development stage for new and returning shows.

"I'm not sure I'm ready to leave Royal," he said, inflating her hopes once more. "But I've been thinking how much I'd like to take you to all the places I've loved the most, and then I remember you don't want to be away from the ranch."

His comment zipped through her like an electric shock. It was exciting to hear that she wasn't the only one pondering their future. The connection between them seemed to grow stronger every day.

"I've been thinking about that, too," she admitted. "Ever since meeting you, I've realized I need to expand my horizons beyond Texas. Maybe after things are settled with..." She trailed off in horror.

By mutual consent, neither of them had mentioned the oil rights issue during their time together. Chelsea recognized that eventually being on opposite sides of the issue was going to blow up in their faces, but she'd been enjoying Nolan's company far too much to make waves.

Nolan put aside the paper and rolled onto his side, facing her. He took her hand in his and brought her palm to his lips. "I think we both know that the situation between our families is going to get worse.

Heath told me he's doing this for Ashley. She started a foundation before she died, and Heath wants to use the money from the oil rights to fund the charity. He wants her name to be remembered."

"That's a wonderful gesture." Chelsea snuggled against Nolan, buried her face in his neck and breathed in his warm, masculine scent. Just being near him brought her comfort. "Enough talk about families. Let's live in this moment and forget everything else."

"I'm down for that," Nolan said, capturing her lips for a long, lingering kiss. "What do you wanna do today?"

Breathless and giddy, Chelsea grinned. "You."

"I'm down for that, too."

Chelsea quivered as his fingertips drifted along her bare thigh. Immediately desire awakened, and a hot hum of longing throbbed between her thighs. She sighed as he stroked the hair off her neck and nuzzled the sensitive skin below her ear. No matter where the man touched, her body came alive. He took her hand, and she thrilled to the physical connection that sent her emotions spiraling. She loved the way he toyed with her hair. This lightest of touches caused goose bumps to break out on her body.

His hands roamed down her chest, long fingers circling her breasts. Pleasure shot through her as he gently captured her nipples through the thin T-shirt she wore and tweaked with enough pressure to make her gasp. The pain awakened her desire, and Chelsea dug her nails into his sides as he skimmed the shirt off her body and closed his mouth over one tight bud.

She parted her legs and rocked her silk-clad core against the steely length of him. He moaned as wildfire streaked through her veins, setting her on fire. Her breath hitched as he sent his fingers diving beneath the waistband of her panties. He caressed the seam between her thigh and body, tantalizingly far from where she needed him most. Anticipation of his touch made her vibrate. Every fiber of her screamed for him to stroke into her wetness and fill her up. As he continued to deny her, Chelsea squirmed in an effort to show him how badly she needed him.

"Look at me."

Her lashes felt as if they were dipped in concrete as she struggled to obey his command. The heat in his eyes made her feel unique and desirable, as if she was the only woman he'd ever wanted like this. It changed her, turned her on, took her to a place of reckless bliss she never wanted to leave.

"Now say my name," he demanded in a rough voice.

"Nolan."

His smile broke her into pieces and then made her whole again. It was an expression of satisfaction and wicked eagerness. He slipped her panties down her thighs, the silky fabric grazing across her feverish skin, making her burn even hotter.

"You are gorgeous," he murmured. "The most amazing woman I've ever met. And I'm dying to taste you." He shifted downward, sliding along her body. "Spread your legs for me."

Chelsea did as he asked, biting her lip as he set his

hands on her thighs and moved his shoulders between them. She was spiraling up to heaven, and he hadn't even gone anywhere near her. Her breath caught as he bent down and sent his tongue lapping through her wetness. Momentarily blinded by a lightning strike of pure pleasure, Chelsea forgot how to breathe as her entire world narrowed to Nolan and the sensation of his hands, lips and tongue driving her mad.

She sank her fingers into his thick, dark hair, anchoring herself to him as he drove her burning need hotter and hotter still. Nothing had ever felt as true or as real as Nolan making love to her. He transported her to places she'd never dreamed existed. Her hips bucked as he flicked his tongue against her clit and then sucked. Incoherent babble broke from her throat as he slid two fingers into her. She bucked against him, her head falling back as she lost herself in the scrape of his stubble, the softness of his lips and the driving hardness of his fingers.

His name poured from her lips and careened around the walls of the loft. She'd never been so glad that the building was built so well as her climax built and her frantic ramblings grew louder. Then she was coming on his mouth, driven by his tongue into a wild, moaning frenzy as she begged for more, rocking against him, tugging on his hair, writhing harder, faster, panting erratically as she fell off the edge and soared.

She was shaking in the aftermath as he kissed his way up her body and nuzzled into her neck. Belatedly, Chelsea realized she'd never released her death grip on his hair and was shocked at the effort it took to unclench her fingers and send her palms gliding over his bare shoulder.

Despite the rigid length of him pressed against her hip that proclaimed he was ready for round two, Nolan seemed content to let his hands and lips drift over her skin.

"That was amazing," she murmured as his tongue drew lazy circles along her collarbone. "You are incredibly gifted."

His breath puffed against her skin as he chuckled. "Glad you think so."

Being with Nolan made her more deliriously happy than she'd ever imagined possible. This was the relationship she'd longed for all her life. The one that had always seemed so elusive. They connected so perfectly that she was convinced they were soul mates.

Chelsea snatched the thought to her chest, imagining how such a declaration would be ridiculed by everyone she loved. Until meeting Nolan, she hadn't realized how narrow her focus had become. By contrast, Nolan's outside-the-norm experiences fascinated her. He meditated unusual deals, acquired amulets to protect the wearer from harm, spoke three languages and had done things most people only read about.

With the amount of time they were spending together, they both realized their need for companionship had been growing. They'd discussed how their contrasting perspectives about family had led to regrets. He'd admitted that although he'd spent half his life avoiding Royal, he felt guilty about the time he'd lost with his mother and sister, adding that he wanted to mend his relationship with Heath. In response, she'd shared that her competitive nature had put her at odds with her siblings. And she'd begun to realize that by focusing all her energy on the ranch, her work-life balance was skewed.

Chelsea found him a great listener. She shared her passion for her family's long history on the land. She knew he wouldn't truly be able to appreciate what it meant to have deep roots and multiple generations growing up on the same acreage. Although he had grown up on a ranch, unlike his brother, Nolan had no attachment to the land. His values weren't in acquiring and maintaining property but in discovering new places and enjoying experiences. Still, she had hoped that her enthusiasm for growing her family's ranching legacy would persuade him to her side.

Although Chelsea hadn't gone so far as to ask him if he'd be willing to convince his brother to drop the claim, she was certain that he'd been sympathetic when she discussed her fears about how her family's land would be damaged by oil companies drilling on the property. He'd seen the devastation wrought by the deforestation of the rain forests in Brazil.

Yet even as she thought she'd won him to her side, Chelsea wasn't sure his help would matter in the end. According to Nolan, Heath was bulldozing ahead with the claim, and although Nolan contended that his brother wasn't solely motivated by wealth, he hadn't explained what was driving Heath.

Oh, why had her grandfather given the oil rights to Cynthia?

"You're tensing up," Nolan commented, his lips gliding into the hollow between her breasts. "What are you thinking about?"

Although she'd spoken freely about so many of her secret desires and the insecurities she kept hidden, the one thing Chelsea couldn't share with Nolan was her anger with Heath over the situation he'd inflicted on her family. The last thing she wanted to do was create conflict between herself and Nolan over something that wasn't his fault. The fact that both of them would eventually have to pick sides was a dark cloud hanging over them.

So she projected an image that she was fine. Pretended to be strong and confident while, inside, her emotions were a Gordian knot of dread.

And instead of confessing what was at the top of her mind, she tackled something that had been brewing for several days. "Do you think we should come out of the closet, so to speak?"

Nolan lifted his head and arched one dark eyebrow at her. "What do you have in mind?"

"Maybe drinks at the Texas Cattleman's Club." Chelsea let out her breath on the suggestion, relieved that he hadn't balked.

"Followed by dinner?"

"We could…" She trembled as his fingers trailed over her abdomen. Reaching up, she stroked her palm over his shoulder, appreciating the solid muscle beneath his warm skin. "It might kick up a whole lot of dust, but I'm so happy that we're dating, and I want everyone to know it."

Plus, if her family saw how good things were between them, how great they were together, surely they'd come around. Her parents were always telling her they only wanted her to be happy. This would be a quick way to see if that was true.

When several seconds had passed and Nolan hadn't responded, uneasiness stirred. Had she misread their relationship? Maybe Heath didn't know Nolan was dating her and he wanted to keep it that way to avoid conflict.

"Unless you don't want to go public," she said, offering him a way out.

"You have to live here. It's more of an issue for you."

Chelsea wasn't sure how to take his response. He wasn't wrong that she had stronger ties to the community than he did, but should she infer that he didn't care about other people's opinions because they weren't important to him—or because he wasn't planning on being in Royal much longer?

Instead of mulling over the issue, Chelsea decided not to spend any more of her Sunday worrying about what might happen in the future. She was in bed with a sexy, half-naked man who deserved her full attention. Making love with Nolan was a much better use of her energy. Chelsea reached between them and took his erection in her hand, loving the way he sucked in a sharp breath as she circled her fingers over the velvety head. She could deal with the rest of the world later.

With a smile, she bent down and flicked her tongue over the bead of moisture on the tip.

Much later.

Ten

Nolan's phone rang as he slid his Jeep into an empty space in the Texas Cattleman's Club parking lot. He glanced at the display as he shut off the engine and grimaced as he recognized the caller. Lyle Short, a producer for GoForth Studios, had warned him a week ago that the studio was close to green-lighting the latest season of their unscripted series *Love in Paradise*. When Nolan had left LA a couple months earlier, he'd left behind several projects in the development stage that would eventually need his attention. Before heading to Royal, he'd submitted preliminary reports on the reconnaissance he'd accomplished, but none of the studio heads had settled on any locations.

"Hey, Lyle," Nolan said. "What news do you have for me?"

"We reviewed your reports and have decided to locate next season in Bora Bora. Can you meet with us at one o'clock tomorrow? We just forwarded all the specs to your assistant, so you will know what we are looking for."

"About that..." The pressure to immediately jump on a plane and head to the South Pacific constricted his chest like a hungry python. "I'm still in Royal. Things here are a little out of sorts at the moment. How much time do I have before you need the location finalized?"

"By the end of the month." Lyle chuckled. "I guess that's the end of next week. You'll see our notes in what we sent to you. We've made some changes to this season's scenario, so there will be a few more arrangements for you to make."

Nolan cursed silently. "That quick?"

He hadn't been prepared to exit Royal so abruptly. It wouldn't sit well with Heath, who was counting on his support in dealing with the Lattimore and Grandin families. Of course, Nolan wasn't handling his dealings with Chelsea to his brother's satisfaction. Which brought up the other reason he was reluctant to leave Royal at this moment—his connection to Chelsea was growing each day. It was too soon to decide if it made sense to take their relationship to the next level, but if he left now, based on how her relationships had ended in the past, Nolan suspected she'd be resistant to a long-distance relationship.

"What's going on, Nolan? It isn't like you to hesitate."

"I know I've always been the first one on a plane, but my brother asked me to come home to help him out with some things, and I really need more time."

"How much time?" Lyle's frown came through loud and clear.

"A couple months."

"I'm not sure that's going to work for us. What's the soonest you could be available?"

"I'd like to give my brother a heads-up. Can I let you know tomorrow?"

Although Nolan used his brother as an excuse for stalling, he recognized that his reluctance centered on Chelsea. The feelings she aroused in him were too new and too scary for him to speak them out loud.

"Sure. But, Nolan, you've already put in a lot of work on this project," Lyle reminded him. "If you can't meet the deadline, we may be forced to turn the job over to someone else."

"I get it." Nolan didn't feel threatened at all by Lyle's ultimatum. It was the nature of the business that production studios were hog-tied by impossible timelines, tight budgets and the constant pressure to produce the next hot thing. "I promise I'll let you know tomorrow if I'm going to do the job or pass."

"Because I know you and how you work, we can wait until tomorrow morning for your answer." Lyle sounded regretful, as if he sensed that Nolan was going to turn down the project.

"Thanks. I owe you one."

He'd come to a crossroad. He either needed to leave Royal and return to his old life or attempt some sort of hybrid situation so he could stay in town part-time while scaling back his traveling and relying on his staff more. Nolan's gut was telling him he was going to pass on this one. He just wasn't ready to leave Royal. Staying away for so long had done too much damage to his relationship with Heath.

Although he'd made inroads with Heath, the brothers had a long way to go before they could be considered close again. If he left now, he risked alienating his brother again. One thing Nolan had decided in the last few weeks was that he didn't want to keep isolating himself from those he cared about the most.

And then there was Chelsea. He'd never been so preoccupied with a woman before. He wanted to be with her all the time, and when they were apart, he struggled to keep his attention focused on matters at hand. If he left now, he might never find out if they could work. Yet was he being a fool to risk his business for a woman he'd only known a couple weeks?

With uncertainty jangling his nerves, Nolan headed toward the entrance to the Texas Cattleman's Club clubhouse, where he was meeting Chelsea for drinks. Choosing to meet at this particular location meant they were publicly stating that they were seeing each other. Up until now, they'd kept a pretty low profile by going outside the city limits of Royal for their dates. While Nolan was ready to let everyone know he was into Chelsea, he recognized that the decision didn't carry a lot of risk for him. He was a relative stranger in town, and with the exception of his brother, Heath, no one really cared whom he was dating.

Chelsea, on the other hand, had family and friends to answer to. No doubt letting everyone know they were a couple was a greater risk for her. Which was why it had surprised Nolan when she'd suggested they be seen together at the Texas Cattleman's Club. Yet despite his surprise, he was also deeply moved that she didn't want to keep the relationship hidden anymore. That had to mean she was serious about him. Which was why he was so conflicted about the project in Bora Bora.

Riddled with clashing emotions, Nolan crossed the threshold and entered the cool dimness of the lobby. After the brightness outside, he was momentarily blind and paused to let his eyes adjust. A shape blocked his path before he'd fully transitioned, and Nolan stepped aside to let the other pass. To his surprise, instead of walking past, the man stopped and greeted him.

"Here to meet my sister, Thurston?"

Nolan might not have recognized the unfriendly voice, but the question made his identity clear. Vic Grandin, Chelsea's brother. Was this the first of many confrontations with a member of Chelsea's family?

"I am," Nolan replied, maintaining a neutral tone as his instincts warned him to be cautious.

"You know that Chelsea is only dating you to find out what you and your brother are up to about the oil rights."

Vic's words went through Nolan like lightning.

He flushed hot and then cold as the disquiet he'd suppressed these last few weeks awakened with a roar. At a loss for what tack to take as a response, Nolan arched an eyebrow and struggled to keep the hit from showing on his face. If Vic was telling the truth, Nolan had been an idiot to open his heart to Chelsea. Yet their time together had been so perfect. Too perfect?

"Don't tell me you're worried about my welfare." Nolan could see his sarcastic rebuke hadn't shut down the other man. Vic was too determined to make a point.

"I just hate to see a guy get played."

"What makes you think that's what's happening?" Nolan was proud that his voice didn't reflect how Vic's insinuation had twisted him up inside. The gut punch of this exchange with Chelsea's brother had shattered the romantic bubble Nolan had been existing in. "It could be your sister and I are merely enjoying each other's company."

"Maybe you're into her, but Chelsea is all about the ranch. She has no personal life. Doesn't give any men in town the time of day. And then you come along, and suddenly she's taking time off and neglecting her responsibilities." Vic sounded put out by this last part. "Don't get me wrong, it's been great to see her screw up. She's always so organized and efficient. But she always puts the ranch first."

Nolan slid his hands into his pockets and regarded the other man in silence.

"Chelsea always thinks she knows best." As Vic

continued his rant, his bitterness came through loud and clear. "She thinks she should be the one in charge of Grandin Ranch."

"She's right," Nolan replied calmly, seeing his matter-of-fact reply struck home.

"She believes if she's the one who saves the ranch from you and you brother, our dad will be convinced that she should run things."

Taking Vic's words at face value was tricky, but the explanation was too plausible for Nolan to ignore. Given what Chelsea had shared with him about her struggles with her brother over control of the ranch, it made sense that she would do whatever it took to win. Even use Nolan.

"Do you know this for a fact or are you guessing?" Nolan had entertained the same conclusion in the beginning.

"It's a fact. She told my whole family that's what she's doing."

"Maybe she told you that to keep you all off her back about being with me."

"Well, well, well." Vic's hearty chuckle was riddled with mockery. "Looks like she has you good and fooled."

Incensed that by defending his relationship with Chelsea, he'd played into Vic's hands, Nolan ground his teeth. "If that's true, and I'm not saying it is, seems to me that by giving me a heads-up about this, you're making trouble for your sister. You must be nervous that she's going to win."

"The ranch is mine."

This glimpse into the other man's motivation didn't ease Nolan's disquiet. Nor did it make his own regret any less potent.

"Maybe if you spent less time sabotaging your sister and more time working as hard as she does, then you wouldn't have anything to worry about." Nolan saw his retaliatory strike hit home. Not surprisingly, this didn't ease the ache in his own chest. "Now, if you'll excuse me."

Nolan brushed past the younger man and headed toward the bar, but as he walked along the wide hallway, he couldn't help but replay his conversation with Vic. Perhaps both he and Chelsea had started out misleading each other, but somewhere along the line, his emotions had engaged.

He was no longer merely interested in her as a way to help his brother. He'd actually begun to consider what sort of relationship she would want when determining his future plans. Given what was going on between their families, he'd known their relationship would be buffeted by negative outside opinions. Nolan had believed that they could weather the storm together. That their ever-strengthening connection would be the bedrock they could build a foundation on. Now it appeared as if the whole thing had been nothing more than a fantasy.

His steps slowed.

So, if he was being played, like Vic claimed, the question of whether he should stay in Royal or take the job in Bora Bora might have just been answered. It might be smart to get away for a while and clear his head. Suddenly, Nolan found himself veering away from the bar.

Heath would not be happy, but Nolan could make him understand. He would just assure his brother that after the location scout, he would return to Royal. He'd only be gone a few weeks. Surely that would be enough time to sort out his feelings for Chelsea and lead with his head and not his heart.

Convinced he was making the right decision, Nolan retraced his steps through the clubhouse and shoved open the door to the outside. He hit the redial button on his phone. The call rolled into voice mail.

"Lyle, hey, it's Nolan. Things have changed here, so I'm available to head to Bora Bora as soon as I can assemble my team. I'm headed back to LA tonight, and I'll see you at the 1:00 p.m. meeting tomorrow."

Chelsea had dressed with care for her rendezvous with Nolan at the Texas Cattleman's Club. She'd borrowed from Natalie a ruched, off-the-shoulder dress in black that hugged her curves, and paired it with black-and-white sandals. Although Nolan loved when she wore her hair down, he also loved plucking the pins free and sending it cascading around her shoulders. Tonight, she'd fastened the mass of chocolate waves into a free-spirited bun with face-framing tendrils. Big gold hoops swung from her ears, and a gold tennis bracelet sparkled on her wrist.

When Chelsea had suggested she and Nolan meet for drinks and dinner at the social hub for her family, friends and neighbors, she'd been on an emotional high after spending the weekend with him. They'd had an amazing time together, and Chelsea's confidence in their strengthening relationship had led her to feel invincible. As long as they faced all opposition together, she was convinced they could overcome everyone's negative opinions.

Unfortunately, two days later, Chelsea was seeing the situation from a more pragmatic point of view, and the excuse she'd been using with her family—that she was seeing Nolan as a way of spying on him and his brother—was going to fall apart when they saw the fondness Chelsea couldn't hide. So she'd convinced Natalie to join her and Nolan for drinks, hoping that having a third person along would prevent anyone from making a public scene.

She'd thought she was prepared for anything, but Nolan neglecting to show blindsided her.

Natalie's gaze flicked to her watch. "You're sure he knew you were meeting at six?"

"He confirmed this afternoon." Her voice sounded as if it was fraying around the edges. "He always texts me to verify we're on. Even before I told him about how Brandon ghosted me, he was great at touching base. He knows it's a sensitive issue for me."

"It's a little after seven," Natalie said cautiously.

Chelsea was well aware what time it was. She felt the tick of each second like the poke of a needle against her skin. For the last forty-five minutes, her emotions had run the gamut between panic, annoyance and deep hurt. Logically, she knew it was ridiculous to let herself be bothered by his lateness, but Nolan was either on time or early, and if he was running late, he would've let her know. Since he'd confirmed that they were meeting at the Texas Cattleman's Club today, all she could think was that he'd gotten cold feet at the last second. This was a big move for them. Today they were broadcasting to all of Royal that they were seeing each other.

"I'm sure he's just running late," Chelsea said, refusing to entertain that it was anything other than an unavoidable delay.

She was convinced that if he'd been able to, Nolan would've let her know what time he'd arrive. Maybe he was having car trouble and was stranded in a zone with no cell service. There were numerous places around Royal like that. Or he could've been in an accident or damaged his phone. She told herself to be patient. Just because he hadn't yet arrived, and hadn't called to let her know he was on his way or that he couldn't make it, didn't mean anything dire had happened.

"It's weird that he hasn't called or texted," Natalie said, her musing scraping Chelsea's raw nerves. "You said he's really good about staying in touch."

"He really is." Chelsea picked up her phone, hoping she'd just missed the notification of his text. Nothing. "It's possible he lost track of time."

"Sure." Pity flickered in Natalie's brown gaze. "That must be it."

Or should she surmise from his delay that he really didn't care about her? Had his innate charm led her to read too much into all his romantic gestures and the amazing sex? What if she wasn't special to him? No doubt she was the most recent in a string of women he'd hooked up with and moved on from. Since he probably didn't linger in a single place for more than a few days, she wouldn't be surprised if she was his longest relationship ever. Rather than flattered, Chelsea felt ashamed of herself for ignoring all the signs.

"You're really bugging out right now, aren't you?" Natalie was peering at her in concern.

"No. Of course not." Chelsea huffed out a pathetic chuckle. "I mean, he's just running late. No big deal."

"For many people, it's probably not a big deal, but you hate tardiness, and I'm sure you're feeling panicky right about now."

"A little panicky. He's never done anything like this before." But then, she'd only been dating him a few weeks. Shouldn't she have suspected that dating a man who was constantly on the move made for an unreliable relationship? "I'm worried something has happened to him."

"Do you want to message him again?"

"I already sent him a text, but he hasn't responded." Chelsea ground her teeth, fighting her worst instincts. "I'm sure he will when he gets the chance."

"And while we wait for him to reply, why don't we have another drink?"

They'd been sipping red wine, but when Chelsea got the bartender's attention, she ordered a shot of whiskey. Ignoring Natalie's worried frown, she tossed back the entire drink. Her eyes teared up as the strong liquor scorched her throat. She gave an inadvertent cough and blinked rapidly.

"Smooth," she muttered, hitting the bartender with a determined stare and gesturing for another shot.

After the second whiskey, a comforting warmth spread through her body, transforming her agitation into reckless disregard. Damn the man. She'd actually let herself trust him. So much so that she'd opened up her heart. She'd ignored everyone's warnings to be cautious. Instead, she'd plowed straight into danger, confident in her judgment. Which, in hindsight, had been completely idiotic. When had she ever done the right thing when it came to her love life? As shrewd as she could be when making decisions for the ranch, the instant she turned over control to her heart, she stopped perceiving reality and created a fantasy based on what she craved.

"Okay," Natalie said, waving the bartender away when Chelsea tried to order her fourth shot. "I think you've had enough."

With her head buzzing, Chelsea was consumed by a sudden urge to emote. "I really love you. You know that, right?" Although she was feeling fairly foggy around the edges, she maintained enough of her faculties to rationalize that keeping her emotions bottled up had led to the explosive pressure that resulted in her making bad decisions regarding Nolan. Maybe if she'd opened herself up more all along, she wouldn't have been so needy when he entered her life.

"I love you, too," Natalie said, laughter edging her

voice. She put her hand atop Chelsea's and squeezed gently. "I'm really sorry Nolan did this to you."

It just couldn't be happening. He'd seemed unruffled by her suggestion that they take their relationship public. Had she misread him? Worse, had she pressured him? Was that what had caused Nolan's abrupt change in behavior? The logical part of her tried to shut down her overly emotional response to Nolan's absence and his lack of communication. But she'd been here before, geared up for a relationship-changing event, only to be left hanging. Was it any wonder she couldn't slow the torrent of insecurity and doubt that washed away every joyful moment she'd spent in Nolan's company?

"You know, it's fine," Chelsea ground out, resentment racing through her.

The dark emotion exploded outward from her aching heart and speared straight into her insecurities. Ghosted again. And by Nolan. What made it worse was that he knew how sensitive she was to being dropped. She'd trusted him and spilled all her fears and self-doubt.

"I mean, it's not like he and I make any sense whatsoever," she went on, grief making her swing wildly. "He's never going to settle down in Royal, and I'm never going to leave here. Everybody got on my case about why I was seeing him and telling me I was so foolish to get involved. Except I'm not foolish." She jabbed her finger into her chest, bruising her breastbone in the process. "I'm Chelsea freaking Grandin. I was using him to find out what he and his brother were planning about the oil rights. That makes me the smartest woman around."

"Ah, Chelsea." Natalie's gaze had gone past her friend, coffee-brown eyes opening wide in concern.

"I'm never going to get played by any man," Chelsea continued, her rant barreling forward unchecked. Damn the man for messing with her heart. He'd actually made her believe he cared. Bastard. "If anyone's doing the playing, it's me."

"That's good to know," came a hard voice.

As the deep timbre of Nolan's tone cut through the fog of Chelsea's misery, regret blazed through her, dispelling much of her self-pity. Enough remained, however, that she wore a scowl as she turned on her bar stool to face Nolan.

The hard planes of his face had never looked more chiseled as he stood like a statue before her. Only his eyes glittered with reproach, making her heart cower. But instead of apologizing for anything she said, Chelsea tilted her chin and went on the offensive.

"So, you decided to finally show up."

He nodded tersely. "I didn't want to leave town without seeing you in person one last time."

"You're leaving?" She heard herself sounding like a small, disappointed child and cursed. "When?"

"Tonight. I'm flying back to LA. There's a project waiting for me, and I have to meet with the producers to get all the specs before I head out to Bora Bora."

The moment she'd been dreading. He was leaving Royal. Leaving her.

"I guess I shouldn't be surprised. You were bound to go at some point."

"Yeah." A muscle jumped in his cheek as he stared down at her. "Too bad you didn't get what you needed before I left."

For a second, she had no idea what he was talking about, and then she realized that he'd heard her whole speech about how she'd only dated him to find out what he and Heath were up to. She froze in horror. She'd stopped pursuing that angle almost immediately. His company had been too enjoyable for her to jeopardize by scheming.

In the weeks since they'd started dating, she'd recognized that her desire to run the ranch had become so important because it was a substitute for the love she wasn't finding in her personal life. She couldn't control her romantic victories, but she could work damned hard to convince her father to give her Grandin Ranch.

"So, you're done with Royal? You're not coming back at all?"

"I don't know." His gaze raked over her. "I still have some unfinished business here."

Chelsea trembled as a familiar heat burned her up. She loved this man. She'd gone and done the one thing she shouldn't—she'd fallen hard. And now she was going to lose him unless she was brave enough to explain that his not showing up had triggered all her insecurities.

"What sort of unfinished business?" She held her breath and waited for the answer she craved.

"I came back to Royal to help out my brother—"

"Of course. It's all about the claim. All along, I figured that's why you hit on me in the first place. Was it your idea or your brother's?" Chelsea couldn't stop her stupid fear from continuing to push him away. "Did Heath tell you about my terrible track record with men? You probably assumed I'd be easy to charm. And I guess you were right."

Nolan scowled at her. "That's not it at all."

"No?" Chelsea couldn't bring herself to confront him directly. Staring into his gorgeous brown eyes always made her melt inside. She couldn't afford to be weak now. "Seems to me after you struck out with my sister, you decided I'd be easier pickings. And I guess I was."

"I never once saw you as easy pickings. And I never hit on your sister. I approached her with the idea that we should talk about the claim, not because I wanted to date her."

"So you're saying you wanted to date me?" She gave a rough laugh. The ache in her chest grew with every syllable he uttered. "Or maybe getting me into bed was just a side benefit to your scheme."

Beside her, Natalie gasped. Tears sprang to Chelsea's eyes, but she blinked them back. She was saying all the wrong things. They both were. In the deepest levels of her heart, she didn't for one second believe that Nolan had been manipulating her. They were both attacking because they were afraid and hurt. And neither of them was brave enough to stop.

"You're accusing me of scheming after admitting

that the only reason you started seeing me was to use me to get my brother to drop the claim?" His lips twisted into a sneer. "That's really rich."

"So you're telling me that you never once considered I could be useful where your family's claim was concerned?"

"Maybe in the beginning—"

"Ha!" she interrupted, crowing in satisfaction even as his confirmation made her cringe inside.

"I said *in the beginning*," he reiterated. "Once I got to know you, and you explained the potential damage to your ranch, I really didn't want to pursue the claim. I tried to talk to my brother—"

"Stop. Please just stop. None of that matters. You're leaving, and that's all there is to it."

"Chelsea," he began, a deep throb in his voice that touched off a wildfire of sorrow inside her.

"Please don't. Whatever it is you want to say, just don't." Even now, after he'd admitted his true motivation for asking her out, he was still trying to charm her. But it was all lies. "No matter what motivated us to get together, we had fun. Let's just leave it at that. We took a swing and missed. No harm, no foul."

As she spouted platitudes, Nolan's expression grew ever more grim. "I guess we're both a couple of players. We used each other, and neither one of us came out the winner." He held out his hand like some sort of sports competitor.

Chelsea didn't want to touch him. To do so, to feel the warm, strong clasp of his hand around hers, would remind her of every time he'd ever touched her. Of the passion that burned so hot between them. Of how she'd loved waking up in his arms. Of the way she'd started dreaming of a future for them.

"It's a draw." She gripped his hand, squeezing hard as she focused on pretending he was nothing more than a business associate in a busted deal. "Good luck in Bora Bora."

She didn't realize until she was halfway to the exit that she'd left her friend behind. Chelsea was so close to losing it that there was no way she could hesitate or stop. Her heart was slowly shattering with each step she took. As the distance between her and Nolan increased, she was terrified that if she looked back, she wouldn't be able to prevent herself from breaking down. As it was, she barely made it to the ladies' room. Her stomach began to turn as she pushed through the door and scrambled for a stall.

The three whiskey shots came up, acid burning her throat in the aftermath of her encounter with Nolan. Tears stung her eyes while ice raced through her veins, making her shake uncontrollably. Her entire world had just ripped apart. Losing the ranch to Vic wouldn't have hurt a fraction of what she was going through as her relationship with Nolan ended. Chelsea stuffed her fist into her mouth and bit down on her knuckles to stop herself from surrendering to the sobs that threatened.

"Chelsea, are you okay?" Natalie had entered the bathroom without Chelsea hearing the door open.

"Of course I'm fine. Why wouldn't I be?" Her overly perky tone failed to mask the bitterness beneath. She'd spent too much of her adult life being strong and never showing weakness. When it came to the ranch or her personal life, she couldn't bear to let anyone think she was anything other than one hundred percent in control.

This outward show of strength, however, didn't work on Natalie. The two women had shared all the ups and downs of both career and personal lives. Natalie was probably the only person on earth who knew all Chelsea's demons.

"Because for the first time ever, you didn't play it safe?" Natalie suggested, her tone gentle and sympathetic. "You let Nolan all the way in."

And in the process, she'd let herself be blindsided.

"I am such an idiot," Chelsea moaned, resting her head against the cool metal of the stall wall. "Why didn't I listen when everybody told me not to get involved with Nolan?"

"Because you two are the real deal."

"Did you not listen to what he just said?" Chelsea unlocked the stall door and stepped out. She avoided Natalie's gaze and stared at her own reflection. Pale face. Enormous, haunted brown eyes. She looked dazed, as if she'd been kicked in the head by a horse. "It was all just a big game to him. And I made such a fool of myself, thinking we had a future. I'll bet he and Heath had a great time laughing at how needy I was."

Natalie let out a weary sigh. "He didn't much look like a man who'd come to gloat. In fact, while you were talking, before you knew he was there, he looked like he's been hit upside the head with a two-by-four."

"No doubt he was surprised that he'd been played in turn."

"I don't think so. He didn't look angry or chagrined. He really looked devastated."

"Well, he's a good actor. He had me completely bamboozled."

"What if the same thing happened to him that happened to you?" Natalie asked. "What if he started out dating you to see what he could find out about the oil rights and ended up falling for you?"

"I'd be more inclined to believe that if he hadn't declared that's why he'd been dating me."

But her words were sheer bravado. Chelsea wanted to believe that at some point he'd begun to care for her. Surely, after all her dating failures, she wouldn't have slept with him if she hadn't sensed genuine emotion.

"Maybe he was just reacting to what you said to save face," Natalie argued. "The way you did. I mean, it's not like after you went on and on about how you were playing him that he would come clean and admit that he had real feelings for you."

Deep inside she hoped Natalie was right. But as she recalled what he'd said, her confidence shrank.

"No. It's not like that." Chelsea shook her head, locked in the grip of her past romantic disasters. "And it doesn't matter, anyway. He's leaving. I'm staying. It was never going to work."

"That's a load of crap and you know it," Natalie declared. "That man makes you happy."

"So what if he does?"

"If you let him leave without telling him how you really feel, then you are not as strong and brave as I thought." Natalie fixed her with a challenging glare. "So, what's it going to be?"

Eleven

Nolan cursed the impulse that had prompted him to return to the Texas Cattleman's Club in time to hear Chelsea confirm her brother's accusations. After his confrontation with Vic, Nolan had been consumed by the need to get as far away from her as possible, so he'd headed back to his loft and made arrangements for a late-night flight to LA. But as he began to pack, it became pretty obvious that much of what he owned was tangled with a number of items Chelsea had left behind.

His instinct had been to toss everything. In fact, he'd been in the process of stuffing a pair of her jeans into a trash bag when he'd come across the T-shirt he'd bought for Chelsea at the cowgirl museum. Emblazoned on the red fabric was the slogan

Well-Behaved Cowgirls Rarely Make History, and Nolan recalled how she'd sauntered around the loft in the shirt, silk panties and her boots. That memory of her was only one of a hundred that had been burned into his brain like a brand. Her brand. He belonged to her in a way that was permanent and irreversible.

The initial shock following his conversation with Vic had worn off by then. He'd rationalized that Chelsea's brother had been making mischief. What better way to mess with his sister than to interfere with her love life? Especially when she was already extraordinarily vulnerable from being treated badly by the previous men she'd dated.

It was then that he'd decided he couldn't leave Royal without seeing her. In retrospect, he should've texted or called her as he was on his way to the airport. He might've saved himself the pain of hearing her brother's accusation confirmed. She had been using him from the start in an effort to save her family's ranch. As much as Nolan had wished it otherwise, Vic Grandin had not been wrong. His sister had played him and nearly won.

Nolan decided to call Heath to let him know he was heading back to LA. While he waited for his brother to answer, Nolan let himself back into the loft to finish packing. Being on the road as much as he was, he was accustomed to packing light. When he'd arrived in town two months earlier, he'd brought little more than his clothes, his electronic devices and a few personal items. He'd signed a month-to-month lease on the fully furnished loft, which meant there was only a week to go. Even though the project in Bora Bora was a quick turnaround, Nolan wasn't sure when he'd be back in Royal. Or if he intended to return at all.

"Hey," Nolan said when Heath answered. "Just wanted to let you know that I'm on my way to LA to take a meeting with some producers. They want me to head to Bora Bora to scout a location for their upcoming show."

The abruptness of Nolan's decision must've caught his brother off guard, because it took him several seconds to respond.

"How long are you gonna be gone?"

A brusque intensity had entered Heath's tone. Was Nolan's brother recalling the first time the brothers had parted? A time when Nolan had disappeared, not to return until their mom and sister's funeral. He couldn't help but feel a familiar urgent need to escape Royal and clear his head.

Nolan wasn't sure what to say to his brother. Given what had happened with Chelsea, Nolan couldn't promise Heath he was coming back. Avoiding entanglements had kept Nolan from slowing down. He liked adventure and experiencing different cultures, but there was also a part of him of him that knew if he kept moving, it was nearly impossible to make the deep connections that lead to expectations, disappointments and heartache. Look at what he was feeling now. If he hadn't let down his guard and gone all in with Chelsea, he wouldn't feel like his insides were being shredded.

"I'm not sure." Feeling the way he was at the moment, Nolan didn't want to come back to Royal at all, but he also didn't want to disrupt the healing relationship between him and Heath. "It depends on the scope of the project."

"I see." From Heath's stiff response, Nolan could tell that his brother wasn't happy.

"I'll know more after the meeting tomorrow." Nolan hated that he felt guilty about disappointing his brother. Strong emotions like this were the exact thing he usually avoided. Yet he couldn't deny that reconnecting with his brother these last few months had made him happier than he'd been in quite some time. Maybe he could learn to take the bad with the good. Surely it would all balance itself out, and in the end, he would have a stronger relationship with his brother. "Look, I know it probably seems like I'm running out on you, but I really do need to get back to work."

"I thought maybe you'd stay in Royal and join me on the ranch."

For a second, Nolan couldn't breathe. He'd never imagined that Heath would offer up such an invitation. Heath had been managing the Thurston ranch since their father died. He'd never needed or wanted Nolan's help before. Why would he include him now?

"I don't think I'd be any help," Nolan said, unsure what to make of the offer. "I've forgotten more than I ever knew about ranching."

"That may be true, but it's been good having you

around." Heath's admission was another blow Nolan hadn't seen coming.

"It's been good being back here with you," Nolan echoed, his chest tight as emotion swept through him. "Makes me wish I hadn't stayed away as long as I did." Swallowing past the lump in his throat, Nolan fought down anxiety. Ever since his mom and sister had died, he'd been buffeted by an emotional storm. Coming home had stirred it further. Reconnecting with Heath was both a blessing and a curse. He liked feeling as if he belonged somewhere, yet at the same time the old tension between the brothers couldn't be resolved without talking through why Nolan had left in the first place.

"I get that work is taking you away. Don't worry about anything here. I just hope you know that you can come back anytime."

"Thanks. I appreciate your understanding. I'll be in touch."

Nolan ended the call and tossed his cell phone on the bed. The conversation with Heath had briefly taken Nolan's mind off his encounter with Chelsea, but as he emptied the closet and dresser drawer, his mind replayed the statements she'd made.

If asked, he never would've pegged her as someone who played games. She'd always struck him as straightforward, someone who believed in hard work and dealt with people honestly. To hear Vic's insinuations confirmed by her had absolutely blown him away. Maybe if he hadn't trusted her and given her the benefit of the doubt, he wouldn't feel like she'd carved out his heart.

A knock sounded on his door. Since the only person who ever visited him was the one person he didn't want to talk to at the moment, Nolan considered pretending he wasn't home, but no doubt she'd already seen that his car was parked in his reserved spot. So, he opened his door and found Chelsea standing in the hall.

"What are you doing here?" he asked, not bothering to moderate his unhappiness.

"I didn't like the way we left things and wanted to clear the air before you left."

He narrowed his gaze and took her in, recognizing her unsteadiness and trouble focusing. "You've been drinking."

"I was drinking before you showed up," she explained. "It's why I said what I did." Her gaze avoided his. "I didn't mean what you heard."

"So you didn't start dating me because of the oil rights claim?"

"Okay, that part was true. But once I got to know you, I stopped thinking of you as a means to an end."

Nolan heaved a sigh. "Why did you come here?"

"I didn't want you to leave Royal with us on bad terms."

She looked absolutely wretched, and Nolan remembered all the times when she'd let herself be vulnerable with him. When she'd shared the most humiliating, heartbreaking moments she'd been through. Had that all been an act to garner his sympathy? To make him want to cherish and protect her? Nolan no longer trusted her or his own reactions to her.

"What does it matter? I'm leaving and we're over."

She made no effort to hide her wince. "Is that what you want? For us to be over?"

What was she playing at? Nolan scrutinized her expression, seeing frustration and hopelessness. For someone who was usually so forthright, Chelsea was certainly dancing around whatever was on her mind.

"I don't know. After talking to your brother—"

"You talked to Vic?" Her eyebrows crashed together. "What did he say to you?"

Nolan was a little taken aback by her vehemence, until he realized this was a symptom of her fierce struggle for control of the ranch. "Exactly what you told Natalie in the bar. He said you've been playing me all along."

"When did you talk to my brother?"

"I was on my way into the Texas Cattleman's Club to meet you when I ran into Vic. He was pretty convincing." Nolan crossed his arms over his chest and stared down at her. "So much so that I decided to head to LA without saying goodbye."

Chelsea glowered while her hands clenched into fists. "He had no right to say anything to you."

"It took me a little while to realize that he might've been actively trying to cause trouble between us. But imagine how I felt after deciding to give you the benefit of the doubt, to show up and hear you echoing exactly what your brother had told me."

"I was upset. You didn't show up when you said

you would, and you weren't answering my texts. It brought up all the times that Brandon did the same thing before ghosting me entirely. I thought the same thing was happening all over, and I went a bit crazy. I had too much to drink and started spouting stupid stuff."

Nolan braced himself against the misery in her eyes even as his heart lurched. Her acute distress was causing his resolve to waver. He'd been ready to give her a chance to explain, even though logic told him her brother had been completely right.

"All great excuses, but the fact remains that you did date me in order to get information on what Heath planned to do about the oil rights."

"Are you trying to tell me that never crossed your mind when we were together?" Chelsea gave him a skeptical look. "Or that your brother put no pressure on you to spy on me in return?"

"So we're both a couple of opportunists." Nolan refused to feel guilty for his part in the scheme. He'd come back to Royal to support his brother, and he'd done a terrible job so far. Both he and Chelsea had known that one day they would have to pick a side, and today he was choosing Heath's.

Chelsea's warm brown eyes dominated her face, unshed tears making them appear larger than ever. "Does that mean everything you said to me was a lie?"

"No." She was amazing. Beautiful. Brilliant. As the tightness in his throat bottled up the words, Nolan's heart ached for what he was pushing away. "It's just that we landed on opposite sides of a bad situation, and even if we wanted to be together, too many things stand in the way."

"That was true in the beginning, and it's no different now," she agreed. "But we could make it work. I really want to give us a shot. Would you be willing to try?"

Would he? His life was a lot less complicated without her in it. The entreaty in her eyes almost sold him, but the turmoil in his chest was a discomfort he couldn't ignore. Was it possible that a mere hour ago he'd been heading to the Texas Cattleman's Club to declare to the public that he and Chelsea were a couple? He'd been happy at this big step in their relationship. Now, all he wanted to do was get away from her and ease the chaotic emotions roiling in him.

"I have this job in Bora Bora to do." It wasn't any kind of an answer, and from the way her shoulders sagged, it wasn't what she hoped to hear. "I don't know how long I'll be gone. If some of the other jobs come through while I'm there, it could be a long time."

"You sound like you're not coming back." She looked stricken. "Is this the end for us?"

Although Nolan had already accepted that they were finished, he reeled at the finality in her question. Before, he'd been so angry with her that he hadn't considered what being parted from her would truly mean. Now, with his outrage fading, he was at the mercy of all his memories of their time together. No woman had ever burrowed so deep into his heart, and the thought of leaving her behind was a knife twisting in his gut. He'd been ready to change his lifestyle for this woman, to make compromises and plan a future with her. But if he'd learned anything in the last hour, it was that the forces at work to keep them apart were stronger than their desire to be together.

"I guess we're lucky we didn't let ourselves get carried away," Nolan said, doing his best to keep his voice light. "At least this way we can part as friends."

"That's not what I want," she said, frowning as she realized how her statement came across. "I mean, I don't want to be parted from you."

Nolan hardened his heart against her entreaty. "So, you're willing to leave everything behind and come with me?"

Her expression said it all.

"I didn't think so." All of a sudden, he had to get away. From her. From Royal. From the longing that made him feel so empty inside. "I have to get to the airport. My flight leaves in a couple hours." He couldn't control the impulse that compelled him to bend down and place his lips against her forehead. "Take care of yourself, Chelsea."

And then he was walking out the door and out of her life for good.

Twelve

Nolan had never thoroughly scouted a location so fast in his life. Nor could he have managed to do even half of what he accomplished without his stellar staff. They worked tirelessly and seemed unfazed that their boss was being an unusually demanding asshole. Perhaps that was because after filling in his assistant about his legal and personal problems in Royal, he'd made sure his employees understood that his distraction and bad mood had nothing to do with the project or them.

It also helped that he'd bought several rounds in the resort bar where they were staying by way of apology.

Every one of the seven days after arriving in Bora Bora, he'd been beating himself up for how he'd left things with Chelsea. She'd pleaded with him to find

a way to compromise so they could be together, and
he'd been too afraid of his strong emotions to meet
her halfway. Telling himself it would never work and
that he was better off ending things before he was in
too deep was idiotic. He'd never been so miserable.
Usually getting on a plane to an exotic location was
a cure for whatever ailed him. For the first time in
his life, he couldn't wait to get home. And that *home*
meant Royal, Texas, instead of Los Angeles was yet
another hit to his belief system.

Yet what he longed for wasn't a place, but a person. Chelsea. She was the home his heart craved. The
safe haven for his restless soul. Except he'd gone and
blown it with her. The one thing he'd promised himself he'd never do, he'd done. He'd made her doubt
him. Worse, he'd made her feel less than thoroughly
desirable. Even if he returned and somehow convinced her to take him back, that breach of her trust
would always be between them.

All that and more should've convinced him to get
over her and move on, but with each hour they were
apart, he was consumed by the need to run back to
her. He hadn't achieved closure by leaving her behind in Royal. Her refusal to give up her life there
and follow him around the world hadn't settled his
mind about their lack of a future. He kept wondering
what would've happened if he'd given in.

Which was why, after most of the details had been
handled to his satisfaction, he'd turned the project
over to his capable assistant and hopped on a plane
back to Texas.

After landing in Dallas, he picked up a rental car and headed for Royal. Conscious that he couldn't speak his heart to Chelsea without first clearing the air with Heath, Nolan headed to the Thurston ranch. He found his brother in the barn, chatting with his foreman.

Heath looked surprised to see him. "You're back? From the way you talked, I thought you'd be gone for quite a while."

"I was running away again," Nolan admitted. "It seems that after fifteen years, it's something I still do."

"At least it didn't take you fifteen years to come back this time."

"Nope. This time I realized that what's most important to me is right here. I love you." Nolan wished he'd declared himself sooner. "I'm sorry I went away for so long. I want us to be close again." He paused to read Heath's expression, and although his brother was nodding in agreement, he seemed to be waiting for the rest of Nolan's intentions. "But this fight you're in with the Grandins is not for me."

"This is about Chelsea, isn't it?"

"I love her." He'd been tossing those three words over and over in his mind for the last few days, but it was the first time he'd said them out loud to anyone. To his surprise, he felt empowered by the announcement. "Being away from her even for a day has been eating me up. I can't go back to living my life the way it was. I want to be with her."

"How does she feel about that?"

"I don't know. I came to you first. I want to clear the air with us."

"This fight with the Grandins is only going to get uglier," Heath warned. "What if she chooses her family over you?"

Nolan was ready with his answer. He'd thought long and hard about his divided loyalties and planned to go with his heart. "Then I'll have to prove that I'm on her side. I'm always going to choose her."

The silence that followed ate into Nolan's soul like acid. Two months earlier, he'd come back to Royal to fix his relationship with his brother, and here he was shattering their alliance into pieces. This wasn't how he'd wanted things to go. But who could've predicted that he would fall in love with Chelsea Grandin?

"I see."

"I know you need to do this thing for our mom and Ashley, but is it worth doing if it tears apart everything that you have built? The Grandin and Lattimore families combined have so many resources to fight with. Is there some way we could just let it go?"

"I can't. Ashley was ignored and denied her birthright." The pain in Heath's voice rang through loud and clear. "She was a Grandin, and they ignored that."

Seeing the bright light of determination burning in his brother's eyes, Nolan decided it was the years he'd spent away that kept him from picking up the same torch that Heath raised. Both their mother and Ashley were dead. They would not benefit from the money. But Nolan understood that his brother's grief needed an outlet, and funding her foundation with the idea that their sister would be remembered was what Heath needed to heal.

"You're right," Nolan said, "but Mom never did anything about the claim."

"She didn't have the strength to take them on," Heath countered. "But I do."

Heath's fervor was getting through to him. Nolan understood more and more what drove his brother, and yet he couldn't believe that Heath would be happy to destroy the Grandin and Lattimore ranches in order to achieve his goal.

Nolan reminded his brother, "I don't think she'd be happy if we end up hurting someone."

"Someone like Chelsea Grandin?" Heath asked. He didn't seem particularly angry at Nolan's attempts to talk him out of pursuing the oil claim rights. More like disappointed.

"Chelsea. Me. You."

"Nothing's gonna happen to me or you." A muscle jumped in Heath's cheek. "I can't say anything about the Grandins or Lattimores, however."

With his brother's ominous words ringing in his ears, Nolan got back into his vehicle and headed to the Grandin ranch. He didn't spend any energy contemplating what sort of reception awaited him there. Deep in his heart, he knew that he would do everything in his power to convince Chelsea to give their relationship a shot. She deserved nothing less that his all. He'd failed her once. Nolan was determined never to do so again.

* * *

Chelsea sat on her bed, her knees drawn up to her chest, her gaze on her laptop screen, where an image of Bora Bora glowed in all its white-sand, turquoise-blue-water glory.

Nolan had been gone for over a week, and she'd never known such misery. It made every breakup she'd ever gone through pale by comparison. In fact, this was worse than every one of them rolled into a single enormous heartache.

Worse, she couldn't even bring herself to be mad at him for ending things. Even if she'd not succumbed to her insecurities and tried to sound all tough and confident, successfully chasing him away in the process, when Nolan had invited her to come away with him, she'd been too afraid to go.

That moment had tormented her for ten days and nights. She couldn't focus on work or even summon the energy to care that in the midst of her battle for the ranch, she'd stopped fighting. The victory she'd labored long and hard to achieve no longer held any luster. What the weeks of dating Nolan had revealed was that she'd been miserable before he came along. And now that he was gone, her life was an endless, desolate landscape once again.

She'd even considered booking a ticket to Bora Bora to surprise him, but fear of his rejection kept her from acting. The whiff of distrust continued to linger. What if he'd been playing her all along? Unable to shake the anxiety that was driven by her past romantic failures, Chelsea continued to grapple with doubt. Nolan wasn't like the other men. He'd had a good reason for ghosting her at the club. Her fingers dug into the coverlet beneath her. Vic had driven him away with his sly meddling.

Still, she'd been the one who'd overreacted and failed to agree to Nolan's offer when he'd extended it to her. If she'd been brave, they could be happily ensconced in paradise together. Blissful with Nolan sounded better than heartbroken alone. Chelsea's resolve swelled. She pulled her computer onto her lap and opened a new browser window.

As she was evaluating which of the twenty-plus-hour flights would work best, she heard a soft knock on her door frame. Glancing up, she spied her dad standing in the hall and closed the laptop.

"Your mother and I are on our way to the cookout at the TCC," he said, frowning as he took in her mood. "Just checking to see if you want to ride with us."

She'd forgotten all about the party at the Texas Cattleman's Club. The all-day affair included a pool party for the kids, a barbecue and a live band. The idea of having to pretend that everything was fine made her stomach roil.

"I'm not really in the mood to be around people right now," Chelsea said.

"You okay?"

She exhaled slowly, emptying her lungs. "Fine."

Chelsea was surprised when her father didn't accept her answer at face value and retreat. Victor Grandin was a straightforward man with old-fashioned ideas about women. The one he'd married, while not a pushover, embodied the traditional role of wife and mother. In contrast, Layla, Chelsea and Morgan had shown a strong preference for having successful careers and Chelsea was sure their father struggled to understand what drove them.

"I haven't seen you much around the ranch these last few weeks." Victor stepped inside the room and leaned against her dresser. With his arms crossed over his chest, he regarded his daughter with a solemn expression. "Some things have been slipping through the cracks."

On a normal day, this criticism would have sparked her irritation. But with Nolan gone, she couldn't summon the energy to point out just how much she did around the ranch. As long as her father was determined to give Vic control, Chelsea was more like a hired hand. Let him see what happened she stopped making decisions that benefited the ranch. Or maybe he would never appreciate how many of her changes had ended up improving things.

Chelsea shrugged, feeling no guilt for acting like a moody teenager for once in her life. "I guess I've been a bit distracted."

"That Thurston boy?"

"Among other things." Chelsea resisted the urge to throw a pillow. "Mostly I'm tired."

Tired of struggling to gain stature in her father's eyes. Tired of fighting a losing battle for a birthright that should've gone to the one who worked the hardest instead of the one who happened to be born male. Tired of telling herself that there was something wrong with the men she chose to date when she suspected that her stubbornness and ambition were the reasons they abandoned her.

"It occurred to me lately that I haven't taken any time off this year," she continued. "I thought I might go visit a friend of mine in Houston. She and her husband are having a baby, and their shower is next weekend."

"I guess you're due for some time off. You work hard around here."

Chelsea's eyebrows shot up. "I didn't realize you noticed." A month ago this admission would've been the confirmation of her worthiness that she'd craved. Today, all she felt was annoyance.

"I pay attention to everything that goes on around here."

"That's interesting," Chelsea said, in no mood to pull her punches. "Because you haven't been noticing that your son has let Layla and me handle the bulk of the problems that come up around here." Seeing her father's surprise, Chelsea warmed to her topic. "You've basically told him he will be in charge, and he thinks that gives him a free pass when it comes to doing things."

"I haven't noticed."

"You don't want to notice." The frustration she'd used to fuel her campaign suddenly had a new target. "You never want to see that your daughters are better at ranching than your son. Because we want the ranch to thrive, and we are willing to work damned hard to make sure it does."

When her father seemed at a loss for words, Chelsea kept going.

"I was willing to do whatever it took to prove to you that I deserved to be the one you should put in charge. Thinking I could save our ranch, I even went so far as to scheme to convince Nolan to talk his brother out of pursuing the oil rights claim." Chelsea's throat locked up at this reminder that her single-minded drive to win at all costs had cost her a future with the man she loved.

"I take it you couldn't."

Chelsea stared at her father in disbelief. Was that the message he'd taken away from her rant?

"More like I didn't want to in the end. Nolan and Heath don't intend to keep the money for themselves. Heath wants to use it to fund his sister's foundation. To do something wonderful in her name. We shouldn't stand in their way."

She could see her father's disapproval grow as she spoke. Chelsea wasn't surprised that he rejected her declaration of support. Her father had very strong opinions. She's been fighting against them all her life. No doubt, he viewed her as a traitor because she wasn't putting the family interest first. It was difficult to choose between two things she loved so much.

With their families on opposite sides of such a fraught issue, and neither party willing to give, they would never be able to please everyone. A relationship between her and Nolan had been doomed from the start.

His decision to leave Royal and take up his old life had probably saved both of them from even greater heartache. Which probably was a good thing, because Chelsea didn't think she could've survived a pain worse than what she was feeling at the moment.

"I'm sure you're disappointed in me," Chelsea said into the silence that had invaded her room. She struggled against the heavy emotions weighing her down. Her father's opinion had always meant so much to her, and going against his wishes added another layer of sadness to her burden of misery.

"I'm not disappointed in you," her father said, crossing to the bed and sitting beside her. He reached for her hand and clasped it in his warm palm. "Maybe I haven't appreciated your contributions the way I should. It's become pretty apparent these last few weeks just how much you do around here. A lot of things have been neglected. Your brother has had a hard time keeping up with everything on his own. Seems to me that you're an asset I've taken for granted."

Chelsea gave her father a watery smile. "I've been waiting a long time for you to recognize everything I contribute to the ranch."

"Maybe you and I should spend some more time together, and you can give me a better sense of all the things you do."

"I'd like that. Running this ranch is all I've ever wanted to do. But I've sacrificed a lot to win your approval. I think I need to find a better balance." As satisfying as it was to hear her father realize that his son wasn't the perfect choice to run the ranch, dating Nolan had awakened her to the need for fun as well as work in her life.

"Does that mean I'm gonna have to get used to seeing Nolan Thurston around here?"

"No." Chelsea dug her nails into her palms to keep from succumbing to tears. "We're over. He left Royal."

"I'm sorry." And to Chelsea's surprise, her father actually looked like he meant it. "I didn't realize what was between you was serious."

"I don't know that it was for him, but I liked him a lot." Way more than a lot. She'd fallen in love with him.

Her father seized her chin and turned her head until she met his gaze. "He's a fool if he doesn't see what a treasure you are."

"Thanks, Dad." Since Chelsea sensed that she'd made inroads where her father was concerned, she decided she could make an effort. After all, he'd come looking for her and had made the effort to get to the bottom of what was bothering her. "I think I've changed my mind about the cookout. Give me ten minutes to change and I'll meet you outside."

After donning a white lace sundress and her favorite boots, Chelsea tied up her hair in a messy topknot and applied mascara, liner and lipstick. She might be miserable inside, but at least she looked good.

As she neared the living room, she heard the low

rumble of conversation and paused to collect herself before entering the room. She expected to find her parents and maybe her brother—but stopped short at the sight of the man who stood in the foyer.

Thirteen

Nolan hadn't known what to expect when Chelsea entered the room, but he didn't expect the flare of joy mixed with despair that erupted as their eyes locked. She looked sad and tragic, but so beautiful in a white lace dress and cowboy boots. Given that he'd thrown down an impossible ultimatum before he'd walked away, he'd half expected she would immediately show him the door. Instead, she stopped dead, as if she'd seen a ghost. Her shoulders collapsed as she reached her left hand across her body and grasped her right forearm.

"Nolan?" She said his name as if she couldn't comprehend that he was standing in the same room as her. "You're here?"

All too conscious of her parents watching the exchange, Nolan nodded. He couldn't seem to make his facial muscles work. Where he wanted to smile and welcome, all he could do was stare at her like a man possessed.

"I'm sorry I didn't call before showing up, but I was afraid you'd tell me not to come. And I needed to talk to you." Nolan shot a glance at her parents, hoping they would get the hint and make themselves scarce. When they showed no signs of moving, he ground his teeth. "Feel like taking a walk?"

"We are on our way to the TCC cookout."

"I could drive you."

Chelsea seemed to have forgotten her parents were in the room. Her gaze stabbed into him as if she could tear him open and get to the heart of why he'd returned. She looked unsure of the situation, which struck him as odd, because he'd never seen her as anything but completely confident.

"Why are you back?" Chelsea asked, showing no sign of going anywhere with him. "I thought you were supposed to be going to Bora Bora."

"I did." Nolan wanted so badly to cross the room and pull Chelsea into his arms, but he'd messed up with her. "My team is still there. I couldn't concentrate with you so far away. So I came back."

"Oh, I see." But from the subdued tone in her voice, Nolan guessed she didn't see it all. "But if there are still things to do, you must be going back."

"The scope of the project requires me to take several trips over the next few months," he said. "And

I realized I couldn't stand being away from you that long."

"Away from me?" she echoed, frowning. "I don't understand. You gave me the impression we were done."

"I didn't want us to be done," he admitted, taking several slow steps in her direction.

She stared at his chest, refusing to meet his gaze, but didn't back away from his advance. He took that as a positive.

"That's not the impression you gave me. You were pretty clear that you weren't coming back. And if you did, you wouldn't be coming back for me."

"I was confused and angry. Your brother said all those things…" Nolan grimaced, all too aware of their audience. "But I should've trusted you."

He glanced toward Chelsea's parents, who were watching the exchange with avid interest, and willed them to go. He wanted this moment with Chelsea to be for just them. So much needed sorting out.

At last, Victor Grandin seemed to get the hint. He captured his wife's elbow in his hand and steered her toward the front door. "We'll wait in the car." As he passed Nolan, Victor gave the younger man a stern glare and muttered, "You be good to my daughter or I will track you down wherever you may run and make you pay."

Nolan wasn't sure if he was more shocked by the man's threat or the backhanded approval of him as his daughter's suitor. Either way, Nolan knew that regardless of the hurt feelings between them, he had to do whatever it took to win her heart.

In the seconds after he found himself alone with Chelsea, Nolan took stock of the tension in her body language. She seemed equally relieved and unhappy to see him.

"The hour I spent waiting for you in the bar was the worst. You'd never given me any doubts before that moment, and when you didn't call or respond to my texts, I didn't know what to think. I was frantic that something had happened to you. And then my insecurity kicked in, and I convinced myself that I'd pushed you into doing something you didn't want and that you'd left me like everyone else."

"I'm so sorry I did that. It was a dick move on my part. I knew perfectly well how you've been treated in the past, and I never should've disappeared on you."

"No," she agreed, her spine stiffening. "You knew how it would devastate me."

"I'm more sorry than you'll ever know," Nolan declared, reaching for her hand. To his relief, she didn't resist as his fingers curved around hers. She seemed to be fighting herself as much as him. "Leaving you was the biggest mistake I've ever made."

"I think we've both made mistakes."

"Can you forgive me?"

"I think I would do anything to have things back the way they were," Chelsea admitted. "And that terrifies me."

"I don't want you to be afraid to be with me."

"I'm not."

"Does this have to do with the oil rights claim you and your brother are making? If it does, then you should know I've already told my dad that we shouldn't stand in your way. I just hope that we can find a way to make it so that our land isn't completely ruined."

"You did?" Nolan couldn't believe what he was hearing. "Why the change of heart?"

"I got to thinking that it wasn't fair for us to fight you when my grandfather gave your mother those rights fair and square. He must've had a reason, and knowing him the way I do, I'm sure it was a good one."

Despite what should be his success in winning her over, her explanation left him ice-cold. She obviously persisted in believing he was committed to the claim, when in truth the only thing he was committed to was making her happy.

"I really don't care about any of that." He grabbed her by the shoulders and gave her a little shake. "I came back for you. Nothing else. I don't care about the oil rights or some job waiting for me in Bora Bora. All I want is you."

"Me?"

The way she said it ripped into his heart. Here stood a woman who understood her worth, yet she questioned whether anyone else saw her value. She worked so hard to prove she was strong and competent, yet her accomplishments hadn't received anywhere near the recognition they were due.

"You." He took her hands in his and brought them

to his lips. "From the minute I laid eyes on you across that Fourth of July parade, I was smitten. My feelings for you only grew stronger the more time we spent together. You are more fascinating than any exotic location could ever be."

"That's not possible. All I've done is focus on this ranch. It's my all-day, every-day fixation." She paused and bit her lip, glancing up at him from beneath her long lashes. "Or it was until you came along. Now, I realize I'd give up running the ranch to be with you. If that means spending the rest of my life on the road, as long as you were there, I could be happy."

Her willingness to sacrifice her passion made his heart clench painfully. The long flights to and from the South Pacific had given him a lot of time to think. Before leaving Royal, she'd pleaded with him to keep their relationship going, and in a moment of cowardice he'd tossed out a ruthless ultimatum, knowing she'd never agree to leave her world behind to be with him. Yet here she was, being braver than any person he'd ever known. And he adored her for it.

"You wouldn't be happy if you couldn't be here, where you belong, making Grandin Ranch the best in the county. Hell, in the whole state of Texas." Nolan put his whole heart and soul into the next two sentences. "And I'd like to be by your side, helping you with that. If you'll have me."

Her eyes went wide with shock. She dug her fingers into his. "But you left Royal because you didn't want to be stuck here ranching."

"I was eighteen when I ran off to see the world. I

couldn't see a place for myself here. But now, after everywhere I've been, recognizing that there are exciting and magical destinations still to visit, I know that what's here in Royal is all I'll ever want. And that's you."

Chelsea stared at Nolan across the inches that separated them. He was telling her that not only did he intend to give up his claim on the oil rights, but he also planned to side with her and her family. Doing so would put his relationship with his brother at risk. He genuinely seemed ready to do that. For her. For them. Did she need more proof that he loved her?

"I love you," she said, willing to take a risk of her own. "It scares me how much I need you. That's why I was so stupid that day at the Texas Cattleman's Club. I fell into my old patterns of self-doubt when you didn't show up, and I went a little crazy."

"I never should have left you there alone. I knew how much it would bother you, and I was so afraid of how you made me feel that I did what I always do and ran. But it didn't take long before I realized that running didn't make me feel better. In fact, I've never been more miserable in my whole life."

"I think we might find a way to overcome our worst fears if we do it together."

Nolan nodded. "It won't be easy."

"I'm not afraid of a little work, and I don't think you are, either." As Chelsea's resolve grew, her fear and anxiety eased. She trusted the bond between her and Nolan. That her confidence in him had developed despite the trouble between their families meant their connection was real and strong. "As long as I have you by my side, nothing else can hurt me."

"Not even if your father decides to let your brother run the ranch?"

A month earlier Nolan's question would've sparked hot emotion. Now, she saw her obsession with running the ranch as a distraction from loneliness and disappointment. She'd longed for someone to share her dreams with, not understanding that she'd lost sight of what made her happy.

"Once you and I began dating, I started to realize that I've sacrificed far too much to my ambition. I can't imagine ever not being a part of running the ranch, but I've focused too hard on changing my father's mind. It led me to think it would somehow be all right to manipulate you into turning on Heath. I'm ashamed that I went there. It's not the way I want to be."

As she bared her soul to Nolan, Chelsea felt stronger than she'd ever been in her whole life. He was a beacon of joy and delight. Together they would be a family and, hopefully one day, welcome children.

Yet, even as these thoughts popped into her mind, Chelsea wondered if she was jumping the gun.

Nolan must've seen her concern, because he cupped her cheek in one hand. "What?"

"I realized that once again I'm throwing myself into the future before I've bothered to find out what you see for us. You love to travel. I'd never ask you to give that up. I want us to explore the world, but I want to make babies with you and see them grow up here." She trailed off, unsure if he wanted to have kids. "Wow, that's a lot." She chuckled self-consciously.

"I've been running around the world for a long time, searching for a missing piece to make me feel whole and never finding it." Nolan's thumb grazed her skin, soothing her worries. "Imagine how surprised I was when I came home to the place I'd fled long ago to discover what I wanted was here all along."

When his hand dived into his pocket and produced a small black box, Chelsea's throat locked up. In that instant, she realized she no longer gave a damn about running Grandin Ranch. This man, the love glinting in his dark brown eyes, filled her with a sense of belonging she'd never known.

"I hope I'm being clear enough," Nolan said. "If not, let me state quite simply that I want you. In fact, I'm really glad that you're imagining a future with me, because otherwise this would've been really awkward." As he finished speaking, Nolan dropped to one knee and popped open the box. A sparkling ring featuring a large oval diamond sat nestled on a cushion of black velvet. "Chelsea Grandin, I love you."

Chelsea threw her hands over her mouth, reeling at his words and unable to believe what she was seeing and hearing. "I love you, too," she repeated, the fierce declaration reduced to a hoarse whisper as emotions overwhelmed her.

"I want to spend the rest of my life with you." The hand holding the ring box shook as fierce emotion burned in his gaze. "Will you marry me?"

Chelsea reached down and clasped his hand between hers, feeling her own body trembling in the acute rush of her joy. "Yes. I want us to be together forever."

Nolan plucked the ring from the box and slid it onto her finger. Chelsea could barely see the diamond through the tears gathering in her eyes. And then he was springing to his feet and wrapping her in his arms. He kissed her with blinding passion, his lips moving over hers with possessive hunger. Chelsea tunneled her fingers through his hair and held on tight as they feasted on each other's lips.

At long last they broke apart, chests heaving as they grinned at each other in giddy, stunned joy. They were so lost in each other and the momentous transformation of the relationship that they didn't realize they were no longer alone until someone cleared their throat.

"Looks like everything's okay in here," Chelsea's father said, sounding somewhat bemused.

Chelsea turned toward her father and spied her mother standing just behind him, looking anxious. Her expression cleared as she gazed from her daughter's face to the man who had wrapped his arm around her and held her possessively at his side.

"Better than okay," Chelsea said. She held out her left hand, where the diamond winked on her ring finger, and braced herself for her parents' reaction. "We're getting married."

"Oh, that's wonderful." Bethany Grandin rushed to embrace her daughter, shocking Chelsea to no end.

"All I ever wanted was for you to be happy," she whispered in her daughter's ear.

She was still absurdly perplexed by her parents' easy acceptance of the "enemy" into their midst as her dad hugged her tight. While Chelsea's mother gave her soon-to-be son-in-law a warm hug, Nolan met her gaze. His warm brown eyes and steady smile filled her with a sense of belonging.

As her father hugged her, Nolan seemed utterly at ease as he basked in the glow of her parents' positive reaction to the news. Yet even as she recognized his solidarity with her family, she worried what would be the cost in his ongoing campaign to repair his relationship with his brother. The conflict drew a line in the sand. In order to be together, they would have to choose a side.

While she recognized that Nolan was willing to make that sacrifice for her without hesitation, if the tables were turned and she'd chosen to support Heath and his claim, the loss of her family would've been devastating.

She needed to make sure Nolan was completely at peace before moving forward. Twisting the ring on her finger, Chelsea prepared to take it off at the slightest indication that he would regret his decision to take her side against his brother.

"Are you sure you're okay with becoming part of my family? I know how much you wanted to repair your relationship with your brother."

"Heath is coping with his grief the best way he can, and while I appreciate that he wants to fund Ashley's foundation and create something in her memory, I can't get past the fact that our mother had the oil rights for years and never did anything about them. It seems to me that she wouldn't agree with what he is doing. If my mom wanted us to take something from you, she would've told us the oil rights existed."

While Nolan's explanation made sense, she couldn't help but argue the same thing from her family's point of view.

"Does that mean you'll talk to your brother on our behalf?" Victor asked before Chelsea could speak her mind.

"Absolutely not," Chelsea answered for him. She wrapped her arm around Nolan's waist and faced her parents. "Grandpa and Augustus granted Cynthia those oil rights. None of us understand why, but the fact is they did. The Thurstons are legally entitled to do whatever they want with them. Neither Nolan nor I will have anything more to say about the rights. You and the Lattimores can fight it, but from now on, we remain neutral."

"This is your ranch we're talking about," Nolan reminded her. "Your family's legacy."

"This is our life," she countered. They were a team now. It was no longer a situation where they sided with his family or her family. From now on, they would prioritize each other and the family they would one day make together. "As far as I'm concerned, we are what's important. Whatever it takes to keep us strong. That's what I intend to do."

Fourteen

Instead of heading to the Texas Cattleman's Club as planned, Nolan and Chelsea took a little detour to his loft. When Nolan had called from Bora Bora, the landlord told him no one had rented it yet, so the loft was Nolan's as long as he wanted it. After a ten-day separation, they were ravenous for each other and didn't get farther than the closed front door before Nolan had Chelsea up against the wall in a hot, desperate kiss.

In minutes, Chelsea had shimmied out of her panties while Nolan freed his erection, and then he was lifting her up and spearing into her. They drove wildly toward a fast orgasm, each thrust a hungry, frantic attempt to get closer and closer still. He loved how she didn't hold back, how she told him exactly how badly she wanted him. With her hands knotted almost painfully in his hair, her breath coming in short, urgent pants against his face, she proclaimed in words and actions just how much she loved him. Nolan lost himself in her desire, and as she came apart in his arms, he was right there with her.

Afterward, they stripped bare and ran to his bed to start all over again. This time the build was slower and hotter as he relearned every inch of her body with his hands and tongue before sliding home. As she closed around him, tight and wet and warm, she gave out a giant, ragged sigh that lanced straight through his heart.

"Are you okay?" he asked, stopping all movement so he could dust kisses across her eyelids and down her nose.

"Better than okay," she murmured, cupping his face between her palms. "I'm absolutely perfect. Being with you is all I could think about these last ten days, and believing that you were gone forever was…" She shuddered. "I can never go through that again."

"Trust me when I tell you that I'm never going to leave you. You're mine and I'm yours. We belong together, and nothing will ever change that."

That seemed to be everything she needed to hear, because her arms and legs tightened around him and she began moving in a way that made every cell in his body come to life. She was perfect and glorious and Nolan knew he would never tire of making her come.

As much as he would've loved to spend the rest of

the day and night in bed with her, Chelsea received several texts from her family demanding to know where she was and reminding her that she had an obligation to join them at the charity event. After grabbing a quick shower together, they managed to get themselves redressed and out the door.

Before he started his rented SUV, Nolan reached into the back seat and pulled out a long, thin jewelry box. Chelsea's eyes widened as he extended it to her.

"What's this?"

"I'm afraid this is going to be anticlimactic after this." He scooped her left hand into his and kissed the spot where her engagement ring rested. "But I thought you might enjoy wearing it to the party."

She popped open the box and gasped at the bracelet of golden Tahitian pearls that lay upon the black velvet. "This is gorgeous." She lifted the strand and placed them on her wrist. The warm gold color looked fantastic against her tan skin. "Can you help me with the clasp?"

Once the bracelet was fastened, Chelsea gave him an enthusiastic thank-you kiss that very nearly sent them scrambling back to his loft for round three. Instead, she wiped her lipstick from his lips, fixed her makeup and shot him a saucy grin.

"Shall we go face the music?"

Nolan pulled a face and started the engine. "It's not going to be that bad."

"Here's hoping you're right."

The last time he'd gone to the Texas Cattleman's Club, he'd intended to meet Chelsea and proclaim their relationship to one and all. To say things had not gone well was an understatement.

This time, as he strode hand in hand with Chelsea through the members who had gathered to eat barbecue, socialize and enjoy the music, Nolan knew a new confidence and contentment. For the first time since returning to Royal two months earlier, he felt as if he belonged in the community. If this was what the love of a wonderful woman did to a man, Nolan knew he would never mess it up.

"Mom and Dad just told me you two are engaged." Layla had appeared in their path with Joshua in tow. While the men nodded in greeting, Layla's blue eyes bounced from Chelsea to Nolan before landing on their clasped hands. Her mouth dropped open as she spotted the large oval diamond. She pointed at it. "It's true. Wow!"

"We are," Chelsea confirmed. Her broad smile was half smug pride and half amusement as her sister enveloped her in an enthusiastic hug. "Do Morgan and Vic know?"

"They do."

"How'd they take it?"

"Morgan's delighted for you, of course, but Vic…"

Layla glanced over her shoulder to where their brother stood talking with his best friend, Jayden Lattimore. The pair cast speculative glances toward the two couples. After the conversation he'd had with Chelsea's brother, Nolan wondered how Vic would react to the engagement.

"It's the whole oil rights thing," Layla continued,

shooting Nolan a glance from beneath her lashes. "His family. Our family."

Chelsea stepped closer to Nolan and pressed her body against his in a show of solidarity. Her chin rose ever so slightly in defiance. "Nolan and I aren't taking sides," she said. "Eventually he's going to become part of our family. Just like I'll be part of his."

Layla looked stunned. "But the ranch—you know that if an oil company gets the right to drill on our land, it will be ruined."

"I know." Chelsea winced. "But Grandpa knew that as well, and both he and Augustus are the ones who signed over the rights to Cynthia."

Nolan squeezed her hand, offering both sympathy and support. "Heath has his reasons for what he's doing and grief is playing a big role in motivating him, but I don't want to see your family's ranch damaged."

"That's good to hear." Morgan had appeared beside Layla. She scrutinized Nolan a long moment before adding, "Welcome to the family."

Beside him, Chelsea relaxed visibly. Despite her brave words earlier, Nolan knew it was important that her parents and sisters supported her decision to marry him. It was also occurring to him how much of a change the Grandin family would make in his life. Since leaving Royal, he'd not been a part of any family, much less one as large as this. The acceptance from Chelsea's sisters delighted him more than he'd expected.

"I love you," he murmured into her hair.

She tipped her head up, and the smile on her face made his heart soar. "I love you," she murmured back. Lifting on tiptoe to kiss his cheek, she added, "Now, let's get out of here and go do some more celebrating back at your loft."

"You do make the best suggestions," he replied with a grin.

Unfortunately, it took them nearly an hour to extricate themselves from the cookout as word of their engagement spread and more people stepped up to congratulate them.

Now, however, they were finally alone. A flush of color high on her cheekbones matched the hungry fire licking his nerve endings. Nolan kicked the front door shut behind them and took both of her hands in his, slowly backing toward his bed. Halfway there he paused, seeing she had something on her mind.

"You're thinking hard about something," he said.

She pulled his arms around her and rested her cheek on his shoulder. "Are you going to be happy here? I mean, you are used to being on the go all the time."

"Wherever you are is where I want to be. Of course, I'll have to travel for my business, but I have an excellent staff who can do most of the day-to-day operations, and LA is a plane ride away."

She leaned back and gazed up at him. "So, you're really okay with being back in Royal."

"This is your home." The ranch was important to her. Her happiness was important to him. "I want to make it mine as well."

"And I want you to know that I'm going to come with you when you travel." Her eyes glowed with fervent joy. "The ranch can survive without me better than I can survive without you."

"That's also how I feel." He framed her face with his hands and kissed her gently. "When it comes to you, I'm—always and forever—all in."

"We're going to have such an amazing life."

"I can't wait to get started."

* * * * *

Don't miss the next book in the
Texas Cattleman's Club:
Ranchers and Rivals series
Rivalry at Play
by Nadine Gonzalez

#2887 RIVALRY AT PLAY
Texas Cattleman's Club: Ranchers and Rivals
by Nadine Gonzalez

Attorney Alexandra Lattimore isn't looking for love. She's home to help her family—and to escape problems at work. But sparks with former rival Jackson Strom are too hot to resist. Will her secrets keep them from rewriting their past?

#2888 THEIR MARRIAGE BARGAIN
Dynasties: Tech Tycoons • by Shannon McKenna

If biotech tycoon Caleb Moss isn't married soon, he'll lose control of the family company. Ex Tilda Riley's unexpected return could solve his marriage bind—in name only. But can this convenient arrangement withstand the heat between them?

#2889 A COLORADO CLAIM
Return to Catamount • by Joanne Rock

Returning home to defend her inheritance, Lark Barclay is surprised to see her ex-husband, rancher Gibson Vaughn. And Gibson proves hard to ignore. She's out to claim her land, but will he reclaim her heart?

#2890 CROSSING TWO LITTLE LINES
by Joss Wood

When heiress Jamie Bacall and blue-collar billionaire Rowan Cowper meet in an elevator, a hot, no-strings fling ensues. But when Jamie learns she's pregnant, will their relationship cross the line into something more?

#2891 THE NANNY GAME
The Eddington Heirs • by Zuri Day

Running his family's empire is a full-time job, so when a baby is dropped off at his estate, Desmond Eddington needs nanny Ivy Campbell. Escaping painful pasts, neither is open to love, but it's impossible to ignore their attraction...

#2892 BLAME IT ON VEGAS
Bad Billionaires • by Kira Sinclair

Avid card shark Luca Kilpatrick hasn't returned to the casino since Annalise Mercado's family accused him of cheating. But now he's the only one who can catch a thief—if he can resist the chemistry that's too strong to deny...

Finding his father's assistant at an underground fight club, playboy Mason Kane realizes he isn't the only one leading a double life. So he offers Charlotte Westbrook a whirlwind Riviera fling to help her loosen up, but it could cost her job and her heart...

Read on for a sneak peek at
Secret Lives After Hours
by Cynthia St. Aubin

They stood facing each other, the summer heat still radiating up from the sidewalk, the sultry breath of a coming storm sifting through their hair.

Now.

Now was the moment where she would pull out her phone, bring up the ride app. Bid him good-night. If she did this, the past three hours could be bundled into a box neither of them would ever have to open again. He might smile at her secretively every now and then, wink at her in acknowledgment, but that would be the end of it.

If she left now.

"Come up," Mason said.

It wasn't a question. It wasn't even an invitation.

It was an answer.

An answer to her own admission in the elevator. That she liked looking at him. That she could look at him more if she wanted.

That he wanted her to.

"Okay," Charlotte said.

Don't miss what happens next in...
Secret Lives After Hours *by Cynthia St. Aubin,*
the next book in The Kane Heirs series!
Available August 2022 wherever
Harlequin Desire books and ebooks are sold.

Harlequin.com

Love Harlequin romance?

DISCOVER.

Be the first to find out about promotions,
news and exclusive content!

 Facebook.com/HarlequinBooks

 Twitter.com/HarlequinBooks

 Instagram.com/HarlequinBooks

 Pinterest.com/HarlequinBooks

 YouTube.com/HarlequinBooks

ReaderService.com

EXPLORE.

Sign up for the Harlequin e-newsletter and
download a free book from any series at
TryHarlequin.com

CONNECT.

Join our Harlequin community to
share your thoughts and connect
with other romance readers!
Facebook.com/groups/HarlequinConnection

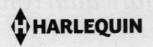

HARLEQUIN

Heartfelt or thrilling, passionate or uplifting—Harlequin is more than just happily-ever-after.

With twelve different series to choose from and new books available every month, you are sure to find stories that will move you, uplift you, inspire and delight you.

HNEWS2021